Frei Betto, born 1944, is a Brazilian writer, political activist, liberation theologian and Dominican friar. He was imprisoned for four years in the 1970s by the military dictatorship for smuggling people out of Brazil. He is still involved in Brazilian politics, and worked for the government of President Lula da Silva as an advisor on prison policy and child hunger. His books have been translated into 23 languages. *Hotel Brasil* is his first crime novel.

HOTEL BRASIL

The Mystery of the Severed Heads

Frei Betto

Translated by Jethro Soutar

BITTER LEMON PRESS
LONDON

BITTER LEMON PRESS

First published in the United Kingdom in 2014 by
Bitter Lemon Press, 37 Arundel Gardens, London W11 2LW

www.bitterlemonpress.com

First published in Portuguese as *Hotel Brasil* by Atica
(1999) and now by Rocco, Rio de Janeiro.
© Frei Betto, 2012

English translation © Jethro Soutar, 2014

This book has been selected to receive financial assistance from
English PEN's "PEN Translates!" programme, supported by Arts
Council England. English PEN exists to promote literature and
our understanding of it, to uphold writers' freedoms around the
world, to campaign against the persecution and imprisonment
of writers for stating their views, and to promote the friendly
co-operation of writers and the free exchange of ideas.
www.englishpen.org

A CIP record for this book is available from the British Library

ISBN 978–1–908524–27–0
eBook ISBN 978–1–908524–28–7

Typeset by Tetragon, London
Printed and bound by CPI Group (UK) Ltd, Croydon, CR0 4YY

Supported using public funding by
**ARTS COUNCIL
ENGLAND**

LOTTERY FUNDED

To Hildebrando Pontes

The novelist is in all of us, and we narrate what we see, for seeing is as complex as anything else.

FERNANDO PESSOA

I

THE RESIDENTS

1   *The Head*

He'd seen it out of the corner of his eye, without meaning to see it. Now he couldn't believe he was seeing what he saw: a head lying dumped on the floor.

He bent over it, confused. He felt a sharp pang in his belly. The palms of his hands became damp with sweat. He forced himself to be strong, to face up to the horror. But he couldn't do it, he couldn't bear to look at the detail. The whole corridor filled with the red of the blood, and he retched.

CONTRASTS

Every day he passed the Arcos da Lapa, a shelter for beggars, dogs and cats, and crawling with rats and cockroaches. Seen from a distance, the miserable spectacle might make a good theme for a watercolour. But Cândido wasn't one for painting, nor was he keen to get closer and linger, to have the repulsive smell impregnate his nostrils, to have his eyes take in the open wounds mottled with flies, the drool running from the limp mouths of drunks, the pregnant mothers scolding ravenous children playing in the rubbish.

The image of his ex-girlfriend popped into his head: her golden hair shining bright amid the congregation;

the way she nibbled her little finger; the intonation of her voice. She didn't draw leering looks from men, nor did she inspire secret envy in women, but she did have certain facets of extraordinary beauty. She listened quietly and attentively to others, had a joyful way of smiling and a shrewd knack for drawing deep significance from the most trivial of facts.

But Cândido had seen both sides of that particular coin and been left mistrustful of the fairer sex. Women could be exuberant on the surface, sensitive, alluring, irresistible. But in private, the petulant genie emerged from among the bed sheets and dishcloths, charm blown away by caprices. Then beauty became a burden, a sack of flesh and bone laid prone on the bed.

His mind was lost in a swirl of memories. What he saw was causing him to lose command of his faculties. He was paralysed by fear, his spirit torn by the stench of death, weighed down by the sense of foreboding. His skin had turned to goosebumps; sweat poured down his temples. He was glued to the spot, as if hemmed in among a crowd. If he could have found the strength, he would have moved, gone back to his room or out into the street, but something prevented him from taking a step. Fear froze him, even as he suffocated in the sweltering heat.

FEAR

As far as Cândido was concerned, fear wasn't a feeling or an emotion. It wasn't the nervous system breaking down and exposing our vulnerabilities and limitations, filling us with insecurity and shame. These were all fear's effects.

He believed that fear's causes lay in social frictions and that these frictions were infused in people's nervous systems. Rio's violence made people prisoners in their own homes, hidden away under lock and key, in flats fitted with security alarms, their windows and balconies covered in grating.

And here was terrifying proof that nobody was spared. Here was the reason the city's inhabitants moved around like soldiers going from trench to trench, hoping not to be struck down between one safe haven and the next. Luxury cars moved about the city like tanks of war: armoured doors, bulletproof glass, electrical security devices.

Cândido felt exposed when he travelled by motorbike, but he couldn't afford a safer mode of transport. This gave him a fatalistic outlook: the belief that nobody dies before their time. *Deus cria, Deus protege.* Cândido wore faith like body armour. This faith helped him not to panic when faced with situations like this one. He hated the contrast between the houses left unlocked in the town he grew up in and the prison-like apartment blocks of Rio, where he now lived. Paying someone a visit in Rio became a ritual: identification, name announced on the intercom, lift unlocked at the appropriate floor, visit confirmed through the magic eye, locks opened one by one with thick, serrated keys.

THE PALE LIGHT OF THE AFTERNOON

Cândido had experienced the same paralysis once before. A schoolmate with a freckly face, fiery hair and a flamboyant way of waving his arms around when telling a story, as if life were a special-effects production that only he could see, had been run over and killed.

One Friday, the boy had left school anxious to get home as quickly as possible. He and his parents were going to spend the weekend in the country at their *fazenda*. Cândido sat with him on the bus. They lived in the same neighbourhood, though the boy's stop was one before Cândido's. Sitting on the left-hand side of the bus, behind the driver's seat, the two boys stared out at the open road. The friend got off and crossed in front of the bus. He disappeared from sight, dragged under the wheels of a van that had been turning the corner. The driver of the van wasn't to know that a child would come rushing out from behind the bus.

It was a cold day, the sky covered in grey clouds. Neighbours and relatives tried to console the boy's parents, who were in a state of total shock. The police took the driver of the van away, as devastated as if he'd killed his own son. The victim lay on the road under a black plastic cover. Onlookers formed a stunned, silent ring around him. Cândido shook, stricken with an angry sorrow, a mixture of hatred and powerlessness. He stood, surrounded by people who had gathered in the pale light of the afternoon in something like a vigil, the particular bleakness of the death having given them all a great sense of reverence.

That day, Cândido wondered about the meaning of life for the first time. Belief in God eluded him.

WITNESS

This was neither the time nor the place for unleashing his demons. Yet Cândido found it impossible to hold back his imagination, to stem the flow of memories brought on by a wave of mixed emotions. Reason withdrew. Tension became overbearing. His heart raced along, pumping out fear. The silence, though interrupted from time to time by the forensics team – who went about their business so carefully that it was as if they feared waking the dead – filled him with uncertainty.

Nervously, he brought the segment of orange he held in his hand to his mouth. The juice flooded his gums, impregnated his taste buds, revived his palate and dribbled down his chin. A pip landed on his tongue. He spat it out with his breath.

He lifted his right hand up to the height of his eyes, the fruit resting between thumb and fingers, and wiped his mouth clean with the back of his left hand. He realized his jaw was trembling with nerves, though he was not the focus of anyone's attention. He knew the size of his own cowardice. And that his shame was no less great. What would the other guests say if they saw him like this, weak at the knees, heart doing somersaults? Yet why this obligation to act tough when everyone knew life consisted of fears? Fear of death, fear of loss, fear of abandonment, fear of ending up forgotten. The same thing had occurred to him once before in the dining room, listening to Pacheco, the political aide, reeling off a string of boasts. Pacheco's thirst for power struck Cândido as being a paroxysm of fear. In Pacheco's case, a pathological fear: being afraid of one's true self and seeking adornments – fame and fortune – to hide that fear from others.

THE WARDROBE

Cândido had hated playing hide-and-seek as a child, ever since he spent a full Sunday afternoon trapped in a wardrobe.

15

It was a neighbour's birthday. The boy's mother iced a cake in the shape of a football while the children played in the yard. "*Um... dois... três...* coming, ready or not!" When the birthday boy opened his eyes and popped his head out from behind the *jabuticabeira* tree, everyone was gone. Cândido had run inside the house and tucked himself in among skirts and blouses, dresses and nightgowns, breathing in the pungent smell of mothballs. He sat there in the dark, waiting for someone to find him.

"*Parabéns pra Você...*" He awoke to the excited singing of Happy Birthday. He tried to get out. The wardrobe door was stuck. He pounded on it and screamed, but nobody came. He felt humiliated that no one had noticed his absence.

Later on, he realized someone had entered the room. He banged on the door and cried for help. The neighbour ran away in her underskirt and bra, panic-stricken, convinced there was a ghost in her bedroom. She called her family for backup, and only then was Cândido set free.

SARCOPHAGUS

The forensics photographed the room in evanescent tones. Cracks in the walls made maps of unknown lands. The open window couldn't hide the smell of damp and mildew, but it did let in some light, a slanted beam that drew whirlpools of dust. From where he was standing by the door, Cândido could see outside to the palm trees on Largo da Lapa and could even make out one of the four snakes on the obelisk, a remnant of Rio's days as the capital, the Prefeitura do Districto Federal.

The room's furniture, mismatched and dilapidated, took

up almost the entire space. Yellowed notebooks spilled out over pornographic magazines on the shelves above the desk. Mineralogy books lay open with holes in their jackets, pages torn in illiterate lines by greedy bookworms. Everywhere dust turned nooks and crannies into cotton fields. Cases lined with cardboard and topped with clear plastic lids showed off emeralds, agates, amethysts, aquamarines, topaz and tourmalines. The gemstones and the open window provided the only sources of light in a dark and dingy shelter.

Sunk into the mahogany bed as if in a sarcophagus, the bloodied corpse looked as if it had been doused in a mixture of red wine and tomato sauce. A hand dangled over the edge of the mattress, seeking help, a ring visible on the wedding finger. The other hand was bent double against the body's lacerated chest, as if trying to fasten a button. Its legs were stretched out rigid and its feet wore shoes with holes in the soles that revealed soiled white socks.

Huddled together in the corridor, the hotel guests whispered laments in whimpering tones. They spoke through gritted teeth, as if not wanting to disturb the deceased, and looked through slit eyes, so as not to meet the gaze of the forensics. They stood shyly before the gaping nakedness of the corpse. They saw without discerning, looked without observing.

The head was still on the floor, its face turned towards the door. Its thin hair was gloopy with blood. Its eyes had been gouged out. Its mouth bore the mocking smile of a man enjoying his own pain. A mask of Mephistopheles.

The contrast between the headless body on the blood-soaked sheets and the head on the wooden floorboards of the corridor struck Cândido as being especially horrid, as if the former were somehow more dead than the latter. He couldn't help thinking of John the Baptist, head on a platter, redeemed by the glory of martyrdom.

LA GIOCONDA'S SMILE

The killer left no trace, no evidence of the murder weapon, not a single clue that might explain the cold-blooded decapitation. Though conclusively dead, the corpse was alive with mysteries.

According to the forensics, the victim died from a stab wound to the heart before having his head chopped off. There was no sign of panic on the severed head's face, nothing to indicate a struggle. Indeed its Gioconda smile suggested the killer had been received like a friend.

The blow to the heart had doubtless been so fast and precise that the victim hadn't even had time to be surprised. On the other hand, there were signs that the beheading had been a slow and laborious process, one performed using a blade considerably larger than a penknife but not as big as a machete. The cut was uneven, as is found on animals skinned and quartered with a blunt knife.

Cândido stood in the doorway, distraught, his mouth plugged by a slice of orange, unable to take his eyes off the scene that so drained his spirit. His mind was a mess, his breathing erratic, his whole chest wheezed when he exhaled. His stomach churned, his legs faltered. He wondered whether he was paralysed by affection for the victim or compassion for penitent souls.

He realized he was incapable of feeling reverential about death without the deceased being in a coffin. He needed to see the body's cold face powdered in purple tones, flowers snug around the body, candlesticks on sentry duty. A profane corpse was different. It returned his stare and had a terrible hold over him. He continued to peer curiously down at the head on the floor as he sucked the sweet liquor out of the orange.

2   *The Man with the Stones*

"Can I interest you in any topaz or amethyst?" whispered Seu Marçal, rummaging in his jacket pocket. He pulled out a fistful of gemstones and arranged them on the palm of his hand.

Cândido was in the TV lounge, a few days after he'd moved into the hotel. Apart from the dining room, which joined on to the kitchen, the TV lounge was the only place where the guests occasionally shared the same space, drawn there by the pull of the television, framed in its varnished wooden box. The room's walls were adorned with an engraving of the Egyptian pyramids, a print of a Rio landscape painting by Debret and a dusty indigenous headdress with withered feathers. Sofas and armchairs were upholstered in a pale yellow cotton that was splattered with shoe polish and grease stains. In the middle of the room a frosted-glass console table held metal ashtrays. Light came in through two chest-high windows by day, while at night a ceiling light with a round lampshade was operated by pulling a golden chain cord.

Cândido had noticed the way Seu Marçal had subtly honed in on him. The old hunter was big and clumsy, but lithe when it came to identifying potential prey. He'd bent over backwards to be courteous to the new arrival, offering to serve him at dinner, his fat fingers clasped around the ladle as he slowly slopped *feijão* over Cândido's steaming rice.

Seu Marçal was all ears whenever Cândido talked about the street children, always sat next to him in the communal areas of the hotel. Now he'd finally made his approach, uttered in the honey-tongued tone of a man whose business it was to make money while letting customers think they were getting a bargain.

Cândido didn't fend Seu Marçal off as Pacheco, Rosaura and some of the other guests did. He admired him at a distance, treating him courteously, but avoiding any familiarity that might establish bonds of friendship. Cândido was guarded not out of distrust but because he felt himself to be past the age when two people form an affinity based on mutual respect and acceptance.

His gaze fell upon the jewel the old pedlar had on his finger: a ring with a chrysolite gemstone like a cat's eye; round and multifaceted, it sparkled lime green encrusted in gold.

Without waiting for an answer to his offer, Seu Marçal delved back into his old black jacket, dusty with dandruff, a jacket he never took off, not even on the hottest of days; they'd doubtless have to bury him in it. He produced a small cardboard box and removed the lid to reveal a handful of coloured gemstones on a bed of bright white cotton. Cândido's eyes trembled before a kaleidoscope of temptations.

"They make great presents," said Seu Marçal with a salesman's smile, ever amused by the compulsive craving of the punter.

Cândido kept his eyes fixed on the gemstones.

"I can offer you a very special price," added the old man, trying to keep his voice casual, "between amigos."

Playing the seducer put a twinkle in his eye, like a crystal encased in the deep hollows of a gnarled face, a face framed by the rusty stubble of a beard.

Cândido appreciated the gesture and stretched out a hand to touch the merchandise.

"*Ora*," said Seu Marçal, snapping the box shut, "if you want anything, you know where to find me."

CHIMERAS

Insomniac lodgers roamed the hotel during the small hours. Cândido was no exception. He preferred to stay in at night, unless he had something on at the Casa do Menor or was called out to deal with some emergency. He liked to prop himself up in bed and entertain himself by reading books or listening to classical music, enraptured by Albinoni's sonatas and Bach's suites. Having grown up in the country's interior, where the roofs were low and the mountains high, he found the metropolis and its giant buildings oppressive. He feared being sucked up by the urban maelstrom, like a blind man stranded at the crossroads of two great boulevards.

By day, Cândido travelled around the city on his motorbike. Alert to danger and careful on bends, he punched into gaps with self-assurance, treating body and bike as one, a machine with eyes. But at night he trusted the eyes in his head and not the machine of his body. He didn't think his legs agile enough to walk easily among hurrying passers-by. And he was scared of being mugged.

His room was a haven. Feeling relaxed after a shower, he gave himself over to daydreaming. If the pages of his book turned faster than his head could keep up with, he retired to the TV lounge to watch the hotel's comings and goings.

Madame Larência, hair splashed with dye, passed by restless, out of the door and onto the street, diligently working the nightclubs, the *boates* and *cabarés*, meeting clients and taking orders. Like that of the Paraná rancher who wanted a "fine young filly with a firm rump and bright blue eyes, and a tub of pistachio ice cream". Once she had the order, she went back to the hotel and searched among her mess of papers for the phone number of a girl to suit the client's tastes. The accessories were always the hardest part, like the ice cream. Few *sorveterias* stayed open late at night, and general stores often didn't stock pistachio.

She'd once had to wake up the owner of a *sorveteria* in Jardim Botânico in the middle of the night, as it was the only place that stocked the particular flavour. The shopkeeper's fury was soon relieved by the rancher's generosity.

Make-up retouched, Madame Larência headed out again, a constant back and forth that typically ended only when the Convento das Carmelitas bell announced morning matins.

Marcelo got back late, his jacket pockets stuffed with cans of beer, and plonked himself down in front of the TV. Eyes glued to the late-night film, he exchanged words with sleepy guests as he supped beer and smoked cigarettes. It gave him singular pleasure to tell his select audience things that wouldn't be in the newspapers until the following morning. As if he lived a day ahead of mere mortals.

Almost all the guests consulted him at times of financial crisis, believing that journalism gave him privileged access to secret information, insider knowledge of spikes in interest rates and the strength of the dollar. Pacheco, the political aide, was the only one who wouldn't listen to him. As he muttered to Diamante Negro, "Marcelo scavenges for news: I make it."

Pacheco came in with his tie loose around the neck and headed hastily towards his room, as if there were not enough hours in the day for a man of his importance. He bustled out again a few minutes later, making for one of the phone booths on the corner of Mosqueira and Avenida Mem de Sá. On finding all the telephones broken, he returned indignant.

"We live in a country full of hooligans! Damned *mestiços* and *vagabundos*!"

No one reacted. This was what made the hotel a kind of Areopagus, a self-contained democracy where words bore no correspondence to actions and emotions clashed without shattering the bell jars in which guests guarded their individual selves, their frustrations and sufferings.

Pacheco sat himself down in the TV lounge, his eyes flicking back and forth between the screen and the clock on the wall. Then he got up, left the room and went out into the street again, only to reappear a few minutes later, absolutely outraged:

"It's a jungle out there! There's no sign of a populace, just flora and fauna!"

Pacheco considered it degrading and unjust that he had to queue for the phone booth with transvestites and prostitutes. If it weren't for the urgent nature of his phone calls, which he considered essential to the well-being of the nation, he would never mix with "that riff-raff, who, for want of a brain, show off their behinds". The other guests listened to him without passing comment, for they all occasionally burst forth with pointless rants.

Diamante Negro came back at daybreak. The TV lay silent and cold, replaced by the sound of roosters and other birds from outside. He sat down in the dark room, unbuttoned his shirt to inspect his chest, and plucked out any hairs he found. He nestled Osíris in his arms, kissing the cat on the nose. He closed his eyes to say a prayer to his *orixás*, waiting for a little peace to descend and clear the way to bed. The hotel's silence gave him a deep and comforting sense of freedom.

TRAJECTORY

Cândido and Seu Marçal waited for the last TV news bulletin of the evening. The old guy rearranged himself uncomfortably in an armchair, feeling pinched on all sides. In his right hand, veins protruding like roots from the soil, his fingers fiddled with a toothpick, occasionally lifting it to his mouth to let it dance among the gaps in his teeth.

"I worked in the tax office back home, in a town called Governador Valadares," Seu Marçal was saying, "up until I retired and entered the gemstone trade. I'd buy them up in Teófilo Otoni and sell them down here in Rio, where jewellers and tourists paid a good price. Back then, there was no competition from the forgers and people weren't into costume jewellery. Business boomed just as my wife fell suddenly ill. In a matter of weeks, she'd left this world for a better one. Her death hastened my decision to move here."

Cândido's eyes drifted from Seu Marçal to the telly. The contraption beamed out adverts with no sound. The old guy's attention had been caught by a model who was running semi-naked along a beach in a soft-drink commercial. An advert for a bank appeared. Two Eskimos came out of the bank covered in snow. Seu Marçal was still lustfully chewing over the thighs of the girl by the sea. Cândido thought about Seu Marçal's misfortune, obliged to go on working after retirement. Images washed over his retina without penetrating his mind. Old age… destitution… precious gemstones…

Cândido turned suddenly to the man squeezed into the armchair. Seu Marçal's head was tipped back, his neck stretched, his mouth open in sleep. Cândido yawned, producing a gruff sound of rising vowels. Seu Marçal opened his eyes. To hide his embarrassment he said to Cândido:

"Why don't you take yourself off to bed?"

"I would if I weren't so tired…" replied Cândido. "I won't be able to get to sleep until my head's calmed down. I spent the whole afternoon at a *delegacia* in Copacabana, trying to get two minors released who'd stolen a Nikon off an Italian photographer."

Cândido was recounting the details of the case when Rosaura came in. She sat on the end of the sofa nearest the TV and put her feet up. Her fingers poked through her flip-flops like Andean pan pipes. Her young face told of fatigue. Her eyebrows formed a delicate arc above her nose. Bending at the waist, she leaned forward to pick up the remote, excused herself and turned the volume on. Cândido stopped his story. The news bulletin was beginning with typical fanfare.

Seu Marçal was the sort of person who thought everything he had to say was interesting. It didn't occur to him that others might find his interjections inopportune. Marcelo would mock him and whisper that Seu Marçal had killed his wife "through deafness and auditory exhaustion". As he recalled the journalist's barb, Cândido yawned again and brought a clenched fist up to his mouth. Seu Marçal was becoming animated.

"I always dreamed of living by the sea, watching the *garotas* go by in skimpy bathing suits all day long," he said, his eyes showing a touch of malice as he waited for Rosaura's reaction.

She pretended she was so absorbed in the news that she hadn't heard him.

He went on:

"I like to appreciate the sort of *beleza* that makes your eyes pop out, makes your heart salivate for the bittersweet taste of sin," he said and sighed, as if the effort to fashion metaphors required periodic pauses and deep breaths.

Her legs now tucked under her, Rosaura's body ached from having been on her feet all day, working as a cleaner. She tried to avoid being cooped up in her room at night before sleep had fully taken hold of her. She wasn't good at dealing with her inner phantoms. She carried around a vague sense of fear and toured the hotel in search of company, though without ever striking up conversation. The mere presence of a living soul was enough to soothe her, even if it was only Dona Dinó's cat.

THE APPARITION

As a girl growing up in the country, Rosaura looked after her younger siblings when her parents left for market in the early hours to get their stall set up by morning. She lay on a mattress of dry straw, ears alive to every sound as she tried to get back to sleep. Outside, a harsh wind blew; a bucket fell in the cement laundry basin; a branch broke off from the *amendoeira* tree; cats wailed like newborn babies abandoned in the forest.

Her body would shake and she'd put her head under the sheet and pray: "*Santa Mãe de Deus*, grant me your protection!"

One night, after her parents had left with the wagon laden with vegetables, she was warming up the youngest brother's bottle when she heard a strange noise in the yard. She took the boy his milk, blew out the oil lamp and picked up a machete. Heart racing, she crouched down by the window and peeked out, her eyes fighting the darkness that surrounded the house. A cold sweat broke out on her skin. "*Santíssima Trindade*," she begged, "show me mercy."

She heard the sound of hooves scraping across the ground. She was torn between curiosity and fear. She dragged the plastic table and chairs over to the door. The youngest brother started to cry. The other two slept soundly. She comforted the little one, then stooped back down by the window. She saw the shape of a stallion cut out against the starry sky. Or was it a mare, lost in the night? From the outline alone, she couldn't make out its snout. Then suddenly she could see it better. Judging by its size, it was more like an ass. It trotted around near the orchard and went back behind the house, stumbling into empty bottles. Still clutching the machete, Rosaura guessed the animal's movements by the sounds it made. A hoe fell next to the chicken pen. Once in a while the animal passed by in front of the window, without ever showing Rosaura its face.

Then she got a glimpse of it close up. It was suddenly right there in front of her, its back to the house, the silhouette of its hindquarters to the window. Slowly, the mule turned round, as if it knew it was being watched. Rosaura squinted hard; she could see the animal's body but still couldn't overcome the darkness hiding its head. Then it whinnied and reared up, its front hooves kicking out at the emptiness, steam coming out of its nostrils at the height of a snout that was still hidden in the night. It ran away at a gallop. Once the animal was back in the moonlight, Rosaura finally unravelled the mystery: the mule had no head!

Rosaura was struck down with tertian fever and was delirious for eight days. Not believing her story, her father attributed the illness to panic. But her mother never doubted her. She said that Dona Maia das Mercês, head of the Filhas da Santíssima Virgem, the sisterhood of the local church, had poisoned herself to death when people found out she'd been offering more than just a hearty meal, clean sheets and a few cups of *catuaba* to the priest when he stayed with her to give Mass the last Sunday of every month,

"The punishment for being a priest's woman," Rosaura's mother whispered into her ear, "is being turned into a headless mule."

SLEEPINESS

On hearing Seu Marçal tell of his erotic fantasies, Rosaura lazily opened her eyes, fixed him with a scornful stare, turned back to the image on the screen, shut her eyes, folded her arms, rearranged her feet under her thighs, rolled over to one side and rested her head on the cushion.

Cândido yawned again. He was too tired to pay attention to the pedlar's flourishing prose. Something about diamonds. Cândido stood up, excused himself, bid everyone *boa noite* and went off to bed.

LABYRINTHS

"Anyone seen Marçal?" asked Madame Larência over Sunday lunch.

Her shrill voice made Pacheco wince. Cândido went on chewing, eyes glued to the newspaper held up in front of his face. Diamante Negro pretended not to have heard, occupied as he was with pouring oil on the salad leaves before him. Rosaura stood up and went over to the stove to serve herself another slice of beef. Jorge, the hotel caretaker, busily washed plates. Dona Dinó, the landlady, broke the silence.

"I think he's gone on his travels."

Madame Larência was wearing an enormous blonde wig and multicoloured bangles that dangled from her arms into her food. Her wrinkles were saturated in cosmetics, her eyebrows thick with liner. She had the habit of ignoring everyone present and asking after those absent. She never spoke to the other diners, never even looked at them. If someone said something to her on her right, she responded monosyllabically and turned to her left, cutting the conversation dead. She preferred talking to herself, mixing up subjects, naming people who perhaps only existed in her imagination.

The windows to her world were open only to men whose eyeballs popped out with lust for genitalia. She also allowed herself certain daily frivolities: skin cream; unhinged conversations with her few friends; a browse around the shops and *perfumarias*; a little tawdry television to lighten her sombre mood.

Emotionally senile, she was the sort of person who avoided conversation for fear of being asked impertinent questions. By day, she sought solace in silence and monologues, sitting in the corner stroking Osíris – she thought him such a beautiful cat with his golden eyes – and thinking of ways to perfect the art of seduction.

Marcelo would often get back late from the newspaper and find Seu Marçal slumped in front of the TV, hypnotized by the late night film. The journalist, cigarette hanging from his bottom lip, would loosen his tie, unfold his arms and bellow:

"*Grande* Marçal!"

Seu Marçal would jump up with fright, while Marcelo's greeting reverberated down the corridor, waking the guests nearest the TV room and startling everyone else, provoking an outburst of swearing from Diamante Negro and causing Osíris to open his translucent eyes.

If the night passed without Marcelo's cry breaking the peace, everyone noted Seu Marçal's absence. The travelling salesman who looked like a funeral director made no secret of his frequent trips to Minas Gerais to "replenish stock".

3   *The Cockroach*

Cândido gave his name and flinched when asked his profession.

"I work for a publisher."

He was uncomfortable with the fact that he didn't have a proper job. He lived off sporadic commissions from Editora Hellas and it hurt his pride to admit that he was stuck in the quicksand, the no-man's-land between the formally employed and the unemployed.

INTERLUDE

"Should I avoid mentioning my work with street children?"

"No way, man!" said Odidnac. "That would only lead them to think you were hiding something and young offenders were involved in Seu Marçal's death."

"You're right, Odid."

ALTER EGO

Cândido always talked to himself when faced with awkward situations. He consulted Odidnac, his alter ego, whom he called Odid.

Cândido added:

"I also do volunteer work with street children."

Delegado Olinto Del Bosco smiled sarcastically.

"With young hoodlums, *senhor* means."

Del Bosco, head of the Delegacia da Lapa, was tempted to go further. He would have liked to explain that aiding young offenders actually kept them in a life of crime. Every time the police locked up a boy guilty of petty theft or couriering for drug-traffickers, some NGO would leap into action and make sure the kid was back on the streets in no time.

But Del Bosco didn't want to disrupt the investigation with an argument that had nothing to do with Seu Marçal's murder, so he contained himself.

SEWER

For Cândido, entering a police station was like entering a minefield. Everything made him feel dirty, as if he hadn't washed for months: scribbled notes on walls, photos of missing persons, pages of reports spread out on tables, warped cupboards, dirty corridors, filthy toilets, broken windows, all-powerful policemen. The whole place treated civilians with indifference, until obstinate persistence managed to triumph over the sluggishness of bureaucracy.

Cândido had to proceed with caution. He knew that police logic meant the detective sought to prove innocence rather than establish guilt. He felt his stomach churn. This time he wasn't there to stop children being abused. He had a corpse in his wake and two eyes before him that saw him as a suspect. But Cândido had learned from his work with minors: speak only when required to; keep answers brief; avoid citing names; stay calm.

"Does *senhor* suspect anyone of having a motive to have committed such a crime?" asked Del Bosco.

There was something about the detective that Cândido didn't like. It wasn't just the tyranny, that sense of being above the law by virtue of administering it. The *delegado* was tall and clean-shaven, with grey hairs just beginning to sprout from his temples. He wore a black shirt buttoned up to the collar and a white silk tie. What made Cândido uncomfortable was the way Del Bosco appeared to be acting a role, a role that he occupied in real life.

In fact, Delegado Del Bosco was a great fan of police films. His mind was a whir of killer blows, audacious moves and perfect traps, a rather over-sophisticated archive for someone who dealt with offences that bore no comparison with the labyrinthine plots of cinema scripts.

He was served a daily fare of prostitutes, pimps, counterfeiters, cheap hotels and unimaginative killers. He had no doubt his talent was being wasted in Lapa as he worked his way up the career ladder, biding his time. But if he were a *bandido*, he'd be untouchable, or so he liked to think.

A keen observer of himself, he had loftier ambitions than stabbings, shootings, punch-ups, extortions, car thefts and crude muggings. He longed for a bank safe emptied without the alarm going off; the death of a *senador* in his mistress' apartment; the kidnapping of a millionaire businessman. Del Bosco dreamed of having his photo on the front pages of newspapers, of doing TV interviews on the evening news, of being paraded before the public as the hero who'd managed to solve a crime that would go down in the annals of police folklore. All of which was why he was treating the Lapa beheading as a routine crime that he needed to get out of the way quick smart.

Meticulous in his investigations, time – the doyen of truth – was on his side. He only ever resorted to aggressive methods when he ran out of patience. To hell with scruples.

He'd joined the Academia de Polícia with the military dictatorship in its death throes. In the main building, an inscription on the wall had been considered great sport even among black rookies: *a negro standing still is suspicious, a running one is guilty*. Del Bosco had experienced training exercises in which apprentices were electrocuted and burned with cigarettes, had their heads held under water or their bodies turned upside down and tied to a pole – the so-called parrot's perch. His left arm bore the scar of a wound caused by a colleague who'd been incited to "thrash the *bandido* with a cudgel".

Del Bosco saw himself as a fisherman that fish just couldn't help swimming towards.

HOLOGRAPHIC PHOTO

"What did *senhor* ask me again?" said Cândido, his eyes distracted by a cockroach that had come sneaking out of a light switch on the wall behind the detective.

"Whether *senhor* suspects anyone of committing the murder?"

"*Não.* I haven't a clue who could have done it."

Cândido possibly didn't have a clue what the detective was even talking about, for he felt an itch on his left leg, where the sock met the opening of his trousers. He gave it a twitchy slap with his hand. Cockroaches made him feel pantophobic. The image of the insect grew in the corner of his brain and played with his emotions, until a holographic photo emerged, divided into a mosaic of fragments, each one containing an image of the cockroach.

The detective stood up and laid his sunglasses down on top of the papers on the table. He started to walk from one side of the room to the other, as if to stress his thinking.

"If I were to say that we suspect the crime to be connected with the international trafficking of precious gemstones, I would doubtless only be expressing a hypothesis that had already passed through *senhor*'s head."

No such thing had passed through Cândido's head. He had imagined other things: Seu Marçal as the victim of an eyeball-smuggling mafia who, having snuck down the dark corridors of the hotel, had surprised the pedlar in his room and, after immobilizing him with chloroform, stabbed him in the heart and set about decapitating him, removing his eyeballs with scissors and pincers, before depositing them in a special solution containing essential nutrients.

INTERLUDE

"Or, who knows, man," whispered Odidnac, *"maybe it was revenge for his hand brushing up against one of those girls who shimmy past semi-naked to the beach."*

"True, the old guy was rather fond of a firm bum-bum, but it's probably best to keep quiet about that."

DETAILS

Cândido scratched his head, intrigued. He would have liked to object to being asked to make conjectures when he was neither a policeman nor a relative of the deceased. He cared little whether the victim was or wasn't a link in some supposed international chain. Only one thing intrigued him: why pull his eyes out? Still, he refrained from saying anything. He kept the cockroach under careful surveillance.

"There's incriminating evidence," continued the peripatetic detective, "that the killer nurtured a strong hatred for the victim. We're not dealing with a mere settling of scores here, rather a carefully executed revenge with a strong emotional component. Nobody goes to the trouble of removing a head from a torso, much less extracts the eyeballs, at great risk of being caught red-handed, unless they're compelled to do so by some uncontrollable impulse. I don't know if *senhor* has ever hated a person enough to want to wipe them off the face of the earth, but it's a lion-like feeling, colossal, indomitable. It awakens the killer inside us and gives us extraordinary strength to crush the enemy mercilessly."

"I've never lost my head," replied Cândido, with monk-like calm.

Del Bosco came to a halt as if someone had tipped a bucket of cold water over him. He clasped the back of the chair, raised his eyebrows and said:

"Lost his head... Lost his head..." He stressed every syllable, seemingly talking to himself.

"Maybe the explanation lies in Minas," said Cândido, still monitoring the cockroach, which was now climbing the far wall and heading for the picture that dominated the room – an official portrait of the Presidente da República.

The detective sat back down. He put his right elbow on the table and rested his temple on his clenched fist. Cândido thought it looked as if he was trying to keep his head from coming loose and falling to the floor.

"We've already requested the assistance of the Vale do Rio Doce police force," Del Bosco said. "I'll go up there personally if our preliminary inquiries don't shed any light on the case."

He paused and changed his tone.

"There's something that intrigues me even more than the murderer's cruelty. Other than the eyeballs, nothing was stolen. The killer didn't take a single gemstone, didn't even remove the victim's ring from his finger. There was no sign of struggle in the room. No windows or doors were forced. And the victim didn't fight off his attacker or try to defend himself."

The detective opened an envelope that was lying on the table.

"Take a look at the photos. I've never seen anyone die with such a happy face! Which would suggest he was killed by someone he considered a friend. According to forensics, before having his head chopped off, he was stabbed in the heart with a blade as fine as a stiletto. He evidently received the blow while sitting on the bed. Immediately after that, the attacker cut his head off using a cold weapon, something similar to a sword. Based on the unevenness of the laceration, this operation must have taken at least an hour."

Cândido placed his hand on his own neck in a reflex gesture, then checked on the cockroach's progress: it was calmly crossing *Sua Excelência*'s presidential sash.

"Where was *senhor* at the time of the murder?"

"In my room, eating an orange," said Cândido. "I'd finished dinner and taken the fruit we'd been given for dessert to my room."

"If *senhor* were to draw up a list of suspects, would Diamante Negro and Madame Larência be on it?" asked Del Bosco.

"Why those two in particular?" Cândido replied, managing to contain himself. In different circumstances he would have dared ask: "Is *senhor* prejudiced, perchance?"

The detective stood up again, seeming not to notice the surprise in Cândido's voice, and caught sight of the cockroach climbing *Sua Excelência*'s nose. Inside the picture frame the president looked terrified, paralysed by an alien force and half squinting, as if he could feel the vile creature advancing on his eyes.

With a brusque motion, the *delegado* swung and slapped at the insect. The cockroach fell to the floor, as did the picture itself, smashing into pieces and sending fragments of glass flying across the room.

"*Perdão!*" exclaimed Del Bosco.

Cândido didn't know whether the detective was apologizing to him, the cockroach or the Presidente da República, who lay stretched out on the floor, sporting the smile of a dethroned hero.

The cockroach emerged from the mess in a frenzy, eager to get home right away. It ran round in circles, finding its progress blocked after making short advances and brandishing its probing antennae to sniff out danger and continue its retreat. It bore the trauma of its interrupted ascent and could also sense the disturbing presence of two huge bulks monitoring its progress.

The detective lifted one of his Italian moccasins and

brought the sole down hard on the cockroach, making a sound like a monkey nut being crunched between molars.

Cândido felt a shiver run down his spine and a sick feeling sweep through his mouth. Nevertheless, he was relieved: a living cockroach took up too much space in any room he found himself in.

Del Bosco concluded:

"*Ora*, it's not a matter of prejudice, if that's what *senhor* thinks. I'm a modern man. In this job I hardly ever deal with normal people – Lapa is a hotbed of sexual deviants – and I treat everyone the same. I only have my suspicions about Diamante Negro and Madame Larência because they were the two guests who had business dealings with Seu Marçal. And, as *senhor* is doubtless aware, they do both lead irregular lives."

4   *Sparkling*

"Name?" asked the detective.

"Elias Procópio da Silva," said the suspect, before adding in a contralto voice, "Diamante Negro to my fans."

"Profession?"

"*Transformista.*"

The exact meaning of the term escaped Del Bosco, but he knew it was "something to do with gays". He didn't ask so as not to show his ignorance.

In fact, Diamante Negro was a quick-change artist. He imitated black singers in late-night cabaret shows in Cinelândia, transforming his voice with the same ease with which he changed wigs, sequined ballgowns and glittering jewellery. High heels lent his lankiness a touch of poise and grace.

He'd have passed for a basketball player if it weren't for his camp manners and way of talking. He had a quip ready for every guest, much to Pacheco's annoyance whenever he was the target.

"Pacheco, what do intellectuals and prawns have in common?"

"*Bem,* I suppose it's their noble attire: they both look dapper in dress coats."

"Oh, *minha santa,* it's that their heads are both full of shit."

41

Dona Dinó liked to say that in Diamante Negro's chest "beat a mother's heart". When Marcelo was bed-bound with pneumonia, he found in Diamante Negro a devoted nurse. If Jorge was struggling to keep up with the dirty dishes, Diamante Negro bent over the sink unprompted, humming and swaying as he scrubbed. If Rosaura needed someone to hold the fabric tight as she stitched up a dress, the *transformista*'s nimble fingers could be relied upon to dance around her needles and thread, scissors and offcuts.

Nobody dared show Diamante Negro disrespect. Some feared his acid tongue, others secretly envied his self-assurance. He was true to himself and cared little for what others thought of him. Generous and mocking at the same time, there was a joy in his words and gestures that was absent from his eyes.

Osíris was his best friend at the hotel. The cat would often sneak out of Dona Dinó's room in the middle of the night to go and nestle on one of the guests' beds, and it invariably favoured Diamante Negro's soft linen sheets.

"The cat is an animal that knows its own mind," Diamante Negro would oft repeat. "It's a matter of self-respect: the *bicha* won't sleep with just anyone. I never did see a police cat, but they sure have plenty of dogs."

BOX OF MAGIC TRICKS

When Diamante Negro abandoned Salvador and the family home, he left a letter stuck to the fridge in which he confessed he was tired of pretending to be someone he was not. "Inside me," he wrote, inspired by the lyrics of a bolero, "I'm a mixture of panic, excitement, horror and charm. I burn with desire to taste the world, to sink my teeth into it and then spit it out because I don't swallow."

"I know the flip side of life," he told his brother, who'd come down to Rio to try and coax Diamante Negro home. "Ever since childhood, people have expected the ways of a man from me, but I know I'm a woman. Inside and out. For years I've lived the nightmare of thinking I'm a *maldito* freak of nature. But life's like that box of magic tricks we used to play with when we were little: full of surprises."

His family was indeed surprised by the changes in Diamante Negro (or "Procopinho" as they'd always called him): his new tone of voice; his coarse, limp-wristed hand gestures; the swish of his hips as he walked; the way he'd express indignation by arching his back, placing his hands on his hips, sighing and rolling his eyes, or show indifference with a marked shrug of the shoulders. At school, he'd always shocked teachers and drawn laughter from classmates with his erotic interpretations of children's stories:

"Snow White shacks up with seven dwarfs, Little Red Riding Hood gets into bed with the Big Bad Wolf, Robin Hood gives it to the poor, Cinderella's prince is obviously a paedophile."

He pleaded with his brother:

"My life is a constant conflict: on the one hand, there's what you all want me to be; on the other, there's what I am."

"You're not a woman!" shouted his brother.

"I'm a clone of myself," said Diamante Negro. "I know I'm not a woman. I'm feminine. It's different."

It was a tough apprenticeship, but Diamante Negro managed to tread a new path for himself, one in which all features of the landscape pointed to the same horizon.

"Every man," he was fond of saying, "carries a woman inside him, just as every woman has a man inside her. No one

43

is solely the sex they appear to be. Everyone has a feminine and a masculine side." And then he liked to add: "Even if one side remains forever trapped in the closet."

In him resided the ancient voices of his heritage. As his talent for mimicry grew, he drew upon those voices until his own evoked African gods with its anguish, nostalgia and earthy sound. When he was on stage, he sang not with his vocal chords, but with his guts.

IMPRESSIONS

"Who killed Seu Marçal?" said the detective, staring him in the eye.

"It must have been some pervert," replied Diamante Negro.

"Why a pervert?" said Del Bosco, fighting the urge to burst out laughing at the suspect's mannerisms.

"Because only a pervert would chop off a head."

"And who do you suspect it was?"

"*Não sei.* Maybe the boyfriend of one of those *meninas* he used to lust over at the hotel door."

"Couldn't you have killed him?" said the detective, trying to be intimidating.

Del Bosco privately amused himself by following the directives of the *Manual do Interrogador.* He had the authority to break, at least morally, the backbones of those he questioned. Suspects typically showed up thinking they'd provide proof of their innocence and be on their way in a matter of minutes. But Del Bosco knew that in the confines of the interrogation room, not only was he the referee, he got to choose the rules of the game as well. He derived twisted pleasure from conducting interviews by slowly racking up the psychological pressure: he explored apparent contradictions; insinuated knowledge of facts that were mere bluff; issued threats simply to watch, right there in front of him, the metamorphosis of a civilian losing his composure, confusing his thoughts, stumbling over words, experiencing fear and humiliation.

Del Bosco saw himself as a spider watching a fly from the safety of its web. The fly thought itself somehow superior, but as soon as it touched against the network of threads, it was confronted by the manifest supremacy of the arachnid.

"Me, a murderer, *delegado*?" said Diamante Negro, flabbergasted. "Call me 'queer' or 'homo' or whatever, but, *por favor*, don't confuse me with rat poison."

"Where were you at the time of the murder?"

"At the Galeria Alasca, in Copacabana, rehearsing my new show, *Ferradas, porém felizes*. I'll have to send *senhor* an invitation to the premiere! I imitate the divine Elizeth Cardoso. A whole bunch of *colegas* can confirm that I arrived at the theatre at six in the afternoon and didn't leave until the small hours. My taxi dropped me off at the hotel just as the meat wagon was taking Seu Marçal away. I only just got there in time to say *adeuzinho*."

"Were you friends?"

"It was only me and Larência who got on well with him at the hotel. I've a collection of gorgeous gemstones bought from his fair hand. *Senhor* should see the red fire of the tourmalines! A real showstopper, believe me!"

"But you also sold stones on for him."

"*Ora*, money's tighter than a tranny's truss at a beauty pageant, *delegado*! In the old days a queer was a queer and a man was a man. Today the competition could kill you! Transvestites, gays, drag queens, *transformistas*, bisexuals,

transsexuals, in the closet, out of the closet, passive, active…
A whole fauna of God only knows what!"

"Would Doutor Pacheco have had motives for eliminating
Seu Marçal?" asked the detective.

"Pacheco? He's nothing but a *safado* bootlicker. He starts
drooling the second he sees a bigwig. He must know all there
is to know about crimes against humanity, but I doubt such
a pirate's *papagaio* would be capable of chopping someone's
head off."

"And Professor Cândido?"

"Ah, he I don't know," said Diamante Negro. "He gets
on well with everyone, but he's not friends with anyone.
He's Dona Dinó's *queridinho*: 'Elias, don't touch the soup
on the stove – it's for Professor Cândido.' Argh! I can't
stand all that surrogate mothering! He doesn't seem to
be the one with the Oedipus complex, though; he just
acts himself. Might he be a serial killer? *Não sei*, maybe he
lopped heads off all over Minas. I'm always wary of people
who paint themselves out as the Good Samaritan. *Senhor*
probably thinks that my *colegas* who work the streets are
afraid of drunks and dockers, men with ugly faces and dirty
clothes? Quite the opposite, *delegado*! They're the upstand-
ing ones – pardon the expression. The ones you really have
to mind your behind with are the office types, with their
shirts and ties and leather briefcases, the ones who smell
of cologne. They're ruffians, *delegado*! They treat the girls
like disposable dolls, haggle over the price and then knock
them about – as if the girls are guilty for making them feel
guilty! Professor Cândido loves street children. Why? He
could be a paedophile for all I know. He comes in and then
rushes off again, running to the aid of some young *rapaz*
who's been arrested."

"Might he have contracted one of these boys to bump Seu Marçal off?" said the detective, more interested in compromising Diamante Negro than in uncovering clues.

"I wouldn't rule anything out," replied Diamante Negro, eager to remove himself from the list of suspects. "When I think about how he portrays himself as some kind of guardian angel for those poor *moleques*, I remember what my grandma used to say: 'The devil's an angel too.'"

"And you can confirm that Madame Larência was friends with Seu Marçal?"

"*Sim*, she was. She also sold gemstones for him. But to suspect her would be a sin. Larência has a heart of gold. She's endured so much in life, she'd never make anyone else suffer."

"And Rosaura?"

"Cinderella?! She'll die waiting for her Prince Charming – she hasn't even got a slipper. She's so pathetic she'd have jumped out of her skin if Seu Marçal had said boo to her goose."

"Does Marcelo Braga figure among your suspects?"

"Marcelo is full of himself, *senhor*. A real Queen of Sheba, he loves attention. If he were a killer, he'd have challenged the victim to a pistol fight. Oh, I'd have loved to see that! But, as reality so often trumps fiction, it wouldn't surprise me in the least if that big closet queer had played *futebol* with Seu Marçal's head."

"Does the hotel caretaker strike you as suspicious?"

Diamante Negro rolled his light-brown eyes, uncrossed his legs, kicked out his feet and then crossed his legs again, swapping knees.

"*Suspeitíssimo*. I pity him, I really do. He works like a slave. I never did trust that *dromedário*. But… oh, shut your mouth!"

he exclaimed, covering his lips with his long, thin fingers. "I wouldn't like to point the finger at anybody, *delegado*. I've no proof against Jorge. All I'll say is this, in confidence: he's always seemed very odd to me. He loves spending the whole day cleaning. The only time he stops is when Botafogo are playing."

On realizing the detective was writing down what he was saying, the *transformista* reconsidered:

"But really, *senhor*, if that useless *plasta* can't even kill time, I doubt he'd manage a person."

5   *Under the Skin*

"Profession?"

"Profession?" repeated Madame Larência, buying time to think of a plausible answer. "*Ora*, I work with quality merchandise for gentlemen of good taste, *delegado*," she said. She was trying to come across as likeable to the detective, who was hunched over the table, taking notes. "Or would *senhor* prefer me to say a *cafetina*, a bawd, a pimp – a specialist in loose women, perhaps?" she then added with a good deal of emphasis, for she made no secret of her business activities. She saw herself as a purveyor of white meat just as others sold cakes, clothes or perfume.

THE OFFER

"Don't you want a better future for your daughter?" she asked Doralice's father, in the outback of the Paraíba *sertão*.

"I do want, *dona*. But times be hard and I can't even pay for her schooling. At the last election, a *rapaz* showed up promising studies for the girl in exchange for my vote. I did like he said, but to this day the poor thing's got no more learning than what Grandma taught her. Maybe at the next election…"

"*Que nada*, the next election! Leave the girl with me. I've already raised half a dozen. One more mouth to feed won't make any difference."

"*Meu Santo Padim Ciço*, praise be! Go on, *menina*, and you listen to the *senhora* now, do what she says like she were your own *mamãe*."

When they got to Recife, Madame Larência took the girl shopping.

"Ask the *rapaz* to engrave *senhora*'s name on the back of this here swell bracelet!" said Doralice.

"I'll ask him to, provided you stop talking like a *caipira*," warned Madame Larência. "The bracelet is not swell, it's beautiful."

"And what's my job to be down south?" asked Doralice.

"Public relations," said Madame Larência. "Wealthy and important clients only. All you have to do, my dear, is keep them happy and never say *não*."

REALIZATION

Once in Rio, teeth brushed, hair combed, clothes arranged suggestively, the girl was sent out on her first engagement. She came back complaining:

"He wanted to abuse me."

Madame Larência rolled her eyes, sighed and stroked Osíris's furry back, the cat purring deep in its bowels with appreciation.

"Being abused, my dear, is going hungry in the *sertão*. If you want to go back there then *tudo bem*, I'll buy your bus ticket today. But if you're staying, then learn a valuable lesson: he who pays the piper calls the tune. He's not asking for your soul, just to kiss your face and caress your body. You don't have to like it, just pretend to."

The yellow of Osíris's eyes shone like gold. Occasionally he showed his teeth or licked his paws.

Doralice realized her new life was not all that she'd hoped for:

"Tia Larência, ain't I becoming a lady of the night?"

"We're all of us ladies of the night, my dear. Do you mean a *puta*?"

"I guess so."

"A *puta* offers herself on the street. You're a courtesan: a courted thespian; a desirable woman with a talent for acting."

"I suppose that's all right, then," said Doralice, relieved.

Madame Larência taught the girl table manners: how to sit up straight, browse a menu, open and fold a napkin, use glasses and cutlery. She taught the girl about make-up: how to apply face creams and powders, paint eyelashes, put lipstick on. She taught her how to manage her appearance: the art of choosing the right outfit, wearing perfume and combing hair according to mood and purpose: tied up if you wanted to go about the streets unnoticed; brushed down if you wanted to attract clients at night.

She showed her how to use her eyes to seduce or fend off, express interest or indifference, display tenderness or dislike. She instructed her on how to deceive the gullible, how to get them drunk, induce premature ejaculation, writhe about in fake pleasure, moan in such a way that the onomatopoeia of orgasm resonated as an outpouring of satiated lust.

She described to her the different types of men: the studs, hungry to eat dessert before the main course; the wise guys, wanting to become lifelong friends in the first five minutes and reap the rewards later; the shy ones, who wait for the woman to take the initiative, but subtly, so that they still feel like the subject and the girl the object; the guilty, with special interest in one particular area of the female anatomy – the ears – where they deposit confidences in the hope of compassion; and the exhibitionists, whose sole desire is to parade the girl around bars and restaurants, clubs and theatres, so that everyone notices, and envies, the beautiful nymph adorning their gentlemanly arms.

AUCTION

Once her apprenticeship was complete, Madame Larência put her "north-eastern treasure" up for auction. Doralice was bought by a racketeer who'd made his fortune as a *jogo do bicho* banker. He kept a harem on a *fazenda* out by Cabo Frio, his own private kingdom, where the girls lived for his pleasure and under his protection. The *fazenda* was guarded by a gang of eunuchs, former bookkeepers who'd been caught with their hands in the till and offered a choice of death or castration.

FATALITY

Three years later, Madame Larência was summoned to the morgue. The sheet was pulled back to reveal a corpse with a bullet in the left breast.

"Does *senhora* recognize the body?"

Madame Larência felt her stomach churn. Her face went so pale it showed through her make-up.

"It's Doralice," she babbled. "But how did you know I knew her?"

"She was wearing a bracelet," the coroner said, "with an inscription: *De Madame Larência para Doralice.*"

FURROWS

Consumed by years and men, Madame Larência's face bore the wrinkles of an age she'd yet to reach. She tried to hide them behind cosmetics and wigs, distract from them with jangling jewellery and high heels that clattered down the hotel corridors, but in vain.

The outside of her heart had become encrusted, a shell of furrows circling her soul. But the inside remained intact. It was there that she kept her true self, hidden away like a photo she could take out from time to time to contemplate and remember the real her.

She was raised the youngest child of a typical suburban family. They lived in a yardless semi with poky rooms, a rag rug in the lounge, an upside-down china penguin on the fridge and a glossy colour photo of her parents' wedding day on top of the TV. The front door opened straight onto the pavement of a road cut in two by the rattle of the tram tracks. Bushy *amendoeiras* provided shade, under which people scattered straw chairs on Sundays, sitting back to watch the world go by and look for gossip.

BUD RIGHTS

Olegário left his job as a clerk at the Central do Brasil railway station early that Friday and hopped on a tram. He hung off the sideboard to get some fresh air, just as

53

he always did, but his eyes didn't lust over women in the street like usual, nor did they run over bulges and curves, imagining the flesh beneath blouses and dresses. He was blinded by excitement, an excitement that ate away at his insides. He carried a present wrapped in tissue paper in his jacket pocket, and eagerness wrapped in his heart. Over the course of the week, the image of his daughter had grown to dominate his thoughts. Flesh of his flesh and now in the full flush of spring, the girl would become a woman by his own hand, before some spotty-faced *moleque* got any macho ideas.

It was Larência's fifteenth birthday. Their house was too small to host a party and so they'd hired the church hall for a small sum. Neighbours and relatives brought snacks and sweets, and a renowned confectioner supplied the cake, chocolate icing on top and nuts in the middle. Boys from the school formed a band to bring a little musical cheer to proceedings.

The girl was full of joy in her white dress, a lacy polka-dot number, pink ribbon tied in her hair. She was showered with kisses and presents, though she was surprised to get a gift from her father. It was a bottle of French perfume, bought off a *contrabandista* in Praça Mauá, and Larência couldn't recall an equivalent gesture in her previous fourteen years. She was touched, threw her arms around his neck and gave him a big kiss.

"I'd like you to wear it tonight," Olegário said. "Put some on before going to bed."

At midnight, Olegário waltzed The Blue Danube with his daughter, drawing great applause from all the guests. A dozen other couples joined the dance floor and Larência felt her father's hand reach around her back and squeeze her body close. She put the excess of paternal affection down to drink and it being an emotional day.

Morning was breaking by the time the family returned home. Larência was laden down with presents and overflowing with happiness. She gave her parents a grateful kiss and went to the bathroom to perform her ablutions. She splashed a little perfume on her neck, nipples and navel and wrapped herself in her new white silk nightie, a present from her mother. She went to bed.

She was just drifting off when she felt a heavy body press up against her on the mattress. *Não*, she wasn't having a nightmare: it was a man. Her scream stuck in the arch of her throat when she realized it was only her father, but the heat of his hairy skin made her freeze. Olegário held his hand over her mouth.

"Sweet daughter, I'm going to lay my marker before some young *safado* gets his hands on you," he whispered into the confused girl's ear, as he pulled his trousers down to perform what he considered his paternal right.

IMPLOSION

Alice's looking glass smashed into a thousand pieces, none of them big enough for Larência to recover the image she'd lost. Why wait for a prince if they were all such pigs?

She started to wash five times a day and never looked her father in the eye again. A little later, on the pretext of wanting to live closer to school, she moved in with a cousin who had a house in São Cristóvão.

Deep resentment came first: the anorexia of her insides being eaten out; the pain of having the sticky silk of a broken spider's web replace her spirit; the promise that no man would lay hands on her body ever again. She would live alone, be consumed by time and die celibate.

Months later, her father abandoned the family home to go and live with a girl from the rail network, a typist some twenty years his junior. This did nothing to placate Larência's rage.

Her brother embarked on a military career while their mother fell into deep depression, wallowing in bitterness, shutting herself off from life and waiting for the comfort of death. She stopped seeing friends and never left the house, sitting at home on her own, talking to herself, letting grief pour out from the cracks in her soul and drown her in dejection. She lost her faith in God and in humanity. Every night, once her domestic chores were done, she sat in front of the TV and surrendered to the magical world of the *telenovelas*.

OUTPOURING

At the Clube Monte Líbano carnival ball, Larência showed off her pink and tender body for the first time, a body with a musky freshness that bit women with envy and made men fear their own fantasies.

Hidden behind a Venetian mask, drunk on the music and the beat, and above all the *lança-perfume* poppers, she allowed firm and hairy hands to wander over her flesh and squeeze her breasts, panting mouths to kiss her lips.

On the third day, Lili, the Rua Alice *cafetina*, approached her in the toilets.

"I hold the key that will unlock your dreams," Lili whispered into the girl's ear. "What do you want? A flat? A car? Financial independence?"

Larência thought about her mother, her cousin, her problems. She took hold of her soul and placed it in a secret box, an inviolable safe, and accepted the *cafetina*'s offer. From that day forth, in a stately home up in Laranjeiras, she gave her body to men – not the body she lived, cried and moved about in, but the one which had been raped by her father.

PROFILES

"I was interested in his precious stones," Madame Larência admitted to the detective. "Every time Marçal got back from one of his trips, Diamante Negro and I would huddle round to check out the latest offerings. In a roundabout way, we were Marçal's sales reps. But I haven't the faintest idea who killed him."

"Where was *senhora* at the time of the murder?" said Del Bosco.

"I wasn't at the hotel, *graças a Deus*. I was visiting a friend, the owner of a cabaret in Lapa. I do so hate the sight of blood."

"Would *senhora* say Seu Marçal had any enemies?"

"If he did, they were in Minas. Everyone liked him here. He was a darling."

"What sort of gemstones did *senhora* buy from him?"

"Tourmalines, topaz, amethyst," she said. "Presents for my *meninas*."

The detective sat up straight in his chair. His eyes shone bright and his face seemed stuck rigid.

"Madame Larência, who killed Seu Marçal?" he said with vehemence, clearly frustrated with the lack of leads the statements were yielding.

"How should I know?! *Senhor* is the policeman," she exclaimed, indignation hiding her fear. "It can't have been anyone from the hotel," she added with some conviction.

"What makes *senhora* so sure?"

"Because, my dear, I know them all so well," she said. "Dona Dinó barely has the strength to lift her broom. Jorge, *pobre-diabo*, would be lost without his apron. Rosaura is a rose scared of its own perfume. Marcelo is a bit of a *rapaz* and quite full of himself, but a coward. Professor Cândido is a *zonzo*, too busy burying his head in books and thinking about street kids to notice what goes on around him – I doubt he even knew Marçal existed. Diamante Negro is a soppy-hearted *donzela* who got on well with Marçal. The only one whose beehive I wouldn't take the honey from is Doutor Pacheco."

"Why not?" said Del Bosco, suddenly interested, hoping for a thread to clutch on to.

"He's arrogant and fake. As he has so little self-worth of his own, he tries to borrow it from others. The worst kind of beggars, *delegado*, are the ones who scrounge admiration."

6   *Exiled*

"Name?"

"Rui Pacheco."

"Occupation?"

"Political aide at the Assembléia Legislativa."

With his short curly hair, tortoiseshell glasses, clipped moustache and hooked nose, Pacheco looked like a man without a sense of humour. He was always in a rush and nothing was ever as important as politics. He went to bed only after he'd seen the last television news bulletin of the night and showered and dressed listening to the radio news in the morning. He read the newspaper meticulously, like a palaeontologist studying symbols on a fragment of ceramics, in search of a lost language.

He got involved in student politics at college, joining the resistance against the dictatorship. He could cite standard tracts of Marxism from memory, and did so with great vehemence and authority.

A strict believer in orthodoxy, he was quick to denounce any exegeses that dared challenge the teachings of his gurus. He believed he had been somehow granted the difficult but glorious task of protecting the ideas of Marx and Engels from false hermeneutics.

Yet deep down he knew the magnitude of his own cowardice.

Every time a demo was declared – a guaranteed police confrontation – he tried to duck out of it, alleging some kind of health problem, a pressing rendezvous with a leader of the underground movement, or an urgent appointment "to analyse the bigger picture".

THE DISTANT AUNT

When the students started turning themselves into *guerrilheiros*, swapping slogans for guns, pamphlets for bombs, street protests for bank expropriations and philosophy books for manuals on the armed struggle, the young Pacheco shaved off his moustache, changed the design of his glasses and only ever left the house dressed in a shirt and tie.

His fear of being rounded up in the increasing furore of repression was such that he gathered together the most prized possessions of his library and made for the farmhouse of a distant aunt. There he would write the first great classic work of Brazilian Marxism, exactly what Karl Heinrich Marx would have produced had he lived in Brazil in the Sixties.

The aunt was a prickly woman with a mean stare and short hair that she tucked under a straw hat. She had skeletal arms and leathery sun-baked skin. A childless widow, she diligently spent her days administering the plot of land she'd inherited from her husband. Fruit from the orchard and greens from the vegetable patch, milk from a handful of cows and the sale of a few chickens and eggs, was enough to provide her with a basic subsistence.

She welcomed the boy, the son of a cousin she'd not seen for quite some time, with sincere hospitality, though little genuine enthusiasm. She didn't want to come across as a busybody, so she didn't ask why the lad was swapping the big city for the countryside. He was at an age when inner turmoils could result in strange behaviour. Perhaps he'd felt the earth calling him, as it had her husband, who'd left his office job in engineering to come and plant orange trees. Or maybe an amorous affair had ended in disappointment and required distance and introspection.

She didn't care what his reasons were, but what she couldn't understand was why someone with such poor eyesight sat in the dark all day looking at books. Furthermore, why such a strapping *rapaz* would prove so impervious to her calls for help: to rebuild the fence knocked down by the cow, spread the plastic awning over the greenhouse before the onset of rain, climb the *abacateiro* trees to pick the fruit before it fell and squashed on the ground. At her age, and with her constant migraines, she was no longer able to do the heavy work and would have appreciated a helping hand.

Realizing that straightforward resistance was not going to shut her up, Pacheco adopted a new tactic: he tried to win her over with the strength of his arguments. At table, over a *bolinho de feijão* or *pão de queijo*, chicken and *quiabo* or mincemeat and *angu*, he tried to convince her that a new means of production was set to burst forth and change history. Soon, every human being would be set free from the chains of centuries of oppression. Under a state cooperative, she would no longer have to rush about frightening the cows or harvest the land with her bare hands in the middle of a thunderstorm.

She asked him when such a paradise would reach her side of the valley, and the question met with a long, sagacious lecture that covered the road to revolution, its inevitable triumph and his personal contributions to the field and its theory. This only served to make her headaches worse, and make her lament all the more that, though he was very studious, her first cousin once removed was a waste of space.

Luckily for her, Pacheco decided he was running too great a risk by remaining in Brazil while engaged in such a thorough critical analysis of Marx's oeuvre (despite the fact that the regime's organs of oppression had never shown the slightest interest in him). He climbed aboard a train and was soon crossing the Mato Grosso *pantanal.*

The hardships of travel were lessened by his recalling Marx's trip from Germany to France a century previously, and Lenin's subsequent journey from St Petersburg to Cracow.

EXILE

Pacheco crossed the Bolivian border and reached Santa Cruz de la Sierra, where the vagaries of the soul led him to try cocaine for the first time and think he was Che Guevara reincarnate. From there, Pacheco headed to La Paz, and from La Paz on to Paris via a bumpy flight that convinced him there were potholes even in the sky.

For a number of years he enjoyed his status of political refugee, able to attend lectures by Althusser, rub shoulders with Sartre over lunch at Les Deux Magots and have endless discussions with exiled compatriots. They would start with the general absurdity of the world, move on to predictions of the imminent failure of capitalism and polish off the last bottle of Beaujolais debating the future of Brazil.

Pacheco attended classes at the Sorbonne and enrolled at the École des Hautes Études, and if he didn't finish any of the courses he started, it was because he found the majority of teachers lacked the competence to teach him.

The more he got news from home of the imprisoned, tortured, disappeared and dead, the more he felt guilty for living on the banks of the Seine. He tried to compensate by working deep into the night, drafting *Quatorze Ensaios Críticos*, an epic work that would finally drag the Brazilian left out of its prehistoric political slumber.

THE RETURN

With the dictatorship in its death throes, an amnesty was granted to all exiles. Pacheco was on the first plane home, manuscript tucked away in his suitcase.

Alas, his luggage was lost in transit. He sued the airline, prayed to Santa Rita and tried to jot down from memory a summary of the central themes of his thesis, but all to no avail. His masterpiece was lost for ever, and he became convinced that the lack of a firm theoretical platform was the principal reason Brazilian politics advanced so slowly.

Pacheco, who liked to be addressed as *doutor*, though he was neither a qualified medic nor academic, quickly found a job as a political aide for a new party, one dreamed up overseas in the salons of European capitals.

PROMISES

"Another month or two now and I'll move into my own penthouse apartment," Pacheco would declare from time to time, without any prospect of it ever happening.

"Pacheco, when are you going to stop eating salami and start belching caviar?" teased Diamante Negro.

"Doutor Pacheco, can't *senhor* get me a job as a television actress?" begged Rosaura.

"Talk to Marcelo. He works in the media."

"I already did. He said that *senhor*'s got more influence than him."

"I'll see what I can do. Don't worry, there are elections coming up."

BACK TO THE SUBJECT

"Where was *senhor* at the time of the murder?" asked the detective.

Pacheco scratched his head and rolled his eyes, as if refreshing his memory.

"At a reception at the *palácio*. The *governador* himself can confirm it."

Del Bosco broke into an ironic smile. He saw he was dealing with a man who thought himself above suspicion because he strode the corridors of power. Del Bosco knew his sort well, the way they puffed out their chests to arrogantly enquire: "Do you know who I am?" All the same, the detective decided to avoid getting into a scuffle.

"Does *senhor* suspect anyone of killing Marçal?"

"He must have been involved in some sort of nefarious business," said Pacheco. "He was a strange person. He'd talk about himself without you asking, recount fanciful stories. He saddled up to all of us, trying to sell us his shiny stones. I wouldn't be the least bit surprised to learn that behind his macho appearance, Marçal was a pederast. That would explain the sophistication and the perversity with which he was killed."

Del Bosco didn't care for the suspect's haughtiness. He cleared his throat, as if his next question was stuck in his windpipe, and asked:

"Doutor Pacheco, why the delay in complying with my summons to come in and testify?"

"Apologies, my learned friend," Pacheco said, attempting to justify himself. "But I didn't attend to the summons immediately because I deemed it appropriate first to contact the Secretário de Segurança Publica, with whom I have direct dealings."

"*Sim*, the *secretário*'s aide called me," said Del Bosco. "I'm sorry to so inconvenience *senhor*," the detective added with little conviction, "but I can't do without *doutor*'s invaluable contribution."

"Of course," Pacheco said, although raised eyebrows and a creased forehead gave his discomfort away.

"What was *senhor*'s relationship like with Seu Marçal?"

"My relationship?!" spluttered Pacheco with a rather unedifying smile. "*Ora*, I can hardly remember what he looked like, whether he was tall or short, handsome or ugly – I'm a very busy man. I only go to the hotel to sleep. Why would I have anything to do with a travelling salesman?"

"*Doutor* is an intelligent and insightful man," said Del Bosco, flattering Pacheco's ego just as the *Manual* prescribed. "Who would *senhor* point the finger at?"

Pacheco rearranged his tie and sat up in his chair.

"It just so happens that I'm a very keen reader of Sir Arthur Conan Doyle and Agatha Christie. I've been giving the matter considerable thought. Seu Marçal's death was a hideous crime, but extremely well planned. Among the hotel's residents, I would rule out the obvious ones, the ones you'd expect to be guilty in a trashy whodunnit: Diamante Negro and Jorge, the caretaker. Neither has the stomach for it, and if it had been one of them, they'd have at least stolen Marçal's aquamarines and emeralds, and probably that ridiculous ring he wore on his finger."

"*Doutor* would, therefore, consider," ventured the detective, "Professor Cândido and Marcelo Braga as suspects."

"If I were Hercule Poirot," said Pacheco, "I'd be following both their trails."

"What about the women?"

"They can all be ruled out," said Pacheco emphatically. "Madame Larência is a retired *puta* who earns a living trafficking false affections. Life has been cruel to her and she hasn't the strength left for hating, much less for killing! Rosaura is a *caipira* fool. She spends her whole time begging me to help her become a *telenovela* actress. Dona Dinó is a typical lumpen proletariat. She struck very lucky in inheriting the hotel, but as she has no learning, the place will never amount to anything more than a flophouse."

"And why does *senhor*, so well connected as he is, live in a 'flophouse'?" Del Bosco said, emphasizing each syllable, and more.

The detective immediately regretted his bout of verbal diarrhoea, asking a question which had nothing to do with the interrogation, but it was too late.

Pacheco went red. Shame flushed through his face whenever anyone enquired as to his social standing. His eyebrows lurched forward, shadowing his eyes. He considered living in Lapa to be humiliating and he always found a way of dodging the question when people asked where he lived. He saw himself as having the profile of someone who lived in

Ipanema or Leblon, and many of his acquaintances indeed believed he was the happy owner of a beachfront penthouse suite in Jardim de Alá.

"My apartment is under construction," said Pacheco, stroking his moustache. "I'll move in just as soon as the complex is ready."

"*Senhor* said that if he were Hercule Poirot he'd follow Cândido's and Marcelo's trails. Why?"

Pacheco sat up straight and adjusted the position of his glasses.

"Marcelo is a busybody. He thinks that just because he's a journalist he has the right to stick his nose into everybody's business. Who knows, maybe he was investigating Seu Marçal's role in the contraband of precious stones? Does *senhor* have any idea how much money the country loses every year from the smuggling of gemstones? Over a billion dollars! I've discussed it with the *ministro* —"

"I'm aware of all that," Del Bosco cut in, "and I have no intention of discussing or investigating the contraband smuggling of gemstones. That's the Polícia Federal's job. But from what I can deduce, Marcelo goes about prying into *doutor*'s affairs."

Pacheco blushed again.

"*Bem*," he said, fiddling with the knot in his tie, "not into my personal affairs – he's not quite that impertinent – but his newspaper accused the *deputado* I represent of tripling his wealth since taking office."

"And is that not true?" said Del Bosco.

"It is true, but it was all totally legitimate," said Pacheco defensively. "A congressman's income corresponds with the function he performs in society. Does *senhor* not earn more than an *investigador*?"

The *delegado* preferred to get back to what really interested him:

"And what are *senhor*'s motives for suspecting Professor Cândido?"

"Cândido is a strange guy. He says little, lives locked away in his room, has no proper job, somehow surviving on casual editorial work, and he hangs about with young hoodlums. Does Dona Dinó let him live in the hotel rent-free? Who knows, maybe he supports himself by illegitimate means. I think the reason he gets on so well with the landlady is because they're both esoteric initiates. And as *senhor* surely knows, certain esoteric practices can be very dangerous: black magic, child sacrifice, pins in dolls and so on."

Del Bosco interrupted him, annoyed by all the inconsistent speculation: "And does *senhor* not believe in the supernatural?"

Pacheco bent forward and placed his hands on his knees.

"At most, I believe in two, maybe three saints. If there were a God, *delegado*, Marçal's head would still be attached to his neck!"

7 Jack of All Trades

"Jorge Maldonado," said the suspect.

The hotel caretaker's bright green eyes projected out of a face full of pockmarks. He had long curly hair tied in a ponytail, fixed in a bun behind his neck. He was the hotel's jack of all trades: he fetched the groceries, prepared the meals, washed and ironed the linen, did all the cleaning and performed checks and repairs on the hotel's electrical and water systems.

He slept in a damp room that was only marginally bigger than he was, tucked in among brooms, squeegees, cloths, buckets and tools. He was literate enough to write his own name, but not much more.

Dona Dinó treated him like a serf who had abdicated all basic human rights in exchange for board and lodging. He didn't seem to mind. As long as he got to listen to the radio and go to the Maracanã to watch Botafogo, he never complained.

"Aren't you Juraci *Funga-Funga*'s brother?" said Del Bosco.

"*Sim*, but I haven't seen him for a long time, *delegado*."

"But you did kill Seu Marçal, didn't you?" said the detective, keen to put the pressure on right away.

Jorge turned pale. He squeezed his thick hands together nervously, making his fingers crack. His lower lip trembled as if exposed to the cold and his eyes became iridescent as they welled with tears.

He couldn't believe that he was really there, in a police station. He'd led his whole life determined to avoid trouble with the police at all costs.

THIRST FOR REVENGE

Jorge grew up in Baixada Fluminense, the youngest son of a father who owned a corner-store bar and was addicted to gambling. One night, men came and dragged the father out of the family home. His body was found in a ditch next to the Rio Guandu five days later, riddled with bullets. Pinned to the corpse was a piece of paper with a messy drawing of a skull and crossbones and two letters scrawled in blood: E. M.

The episode naturally left a nasty taste in the mouth, a taste Jorge's older brother, Juraci, refused to swallow.

"The *velho*'s death must be avenged!"

Juraci slipped a Mauser into his belt and went looking for answers, prowling back alleys and street corners that operated on the margins of the law.

As he gradually clogged his nostrils with cocaine, Juraci lost his way in life, along with the thread of the trail that was supposed to lead to his father's killers. To pay off debts, he entered the drug trade, leading gun battles with rival gangs over sales pitches and scratching a dash into the butt of his gun every time he sent someone into the next world.

When eventually arrested, he was dealt a sentence that would require him to live three times over if it were to be fulfilled. Jorge visited him in jail with their mother, until she surrendered to her sorrow, stopped eating, turned to skin and bone and died.

As an orphan, Jorge's visits became less and less frequent, until finally all sense of brotherly feeling evaporated. Yet one thing about Juraci stayed with him for ever: prison life was hell. Even if Jorge's own life had hardly been one of opportunity, it had at least taught him one thing: never do anything that might mean relying on the justice of mankind, for it was merciless to the poor.

PRESSURE

Jorge was shell-shocked. *Ai, meu Deus*, how awful! Could the detective really think it was him?

"*Pelo amor de Deus*, don't say such things," he begged. "Maybe I have nowhere to fall when I die, but I lead an honest life, *delegado*. If I were a *bandido* like my brother, I wouldn't work all day and live in a tiny room full of bedbugs, fleas and cockroaches."

Now here was an easy arrest, thought Del Bosco. Jorge was the typical sort of witness police singled out as potential defendants: no profession, wealth or education; no lawyers, acquaintances or family members to defend them. This was the base material – society's scraps – that they filled the jails with. Del Bosco's authority as a police officer gave him the power to ignore the fine line that distinguished poverty from delinquency, and he never hesitated to use that power whenever public opinion demanded a scalp. Society's sense of insecurity could always be temporarily assuaged by locking someone up, some poor sap condemned by his social standing.

71

Del Bosco exercised his jaw and moved in closer to the suspect. He tugged on Jorge's ponytail and whispered forcefully in his ear:

"Spit it out, then: if it wasn't you, who did top Seu Marçal?"

Jorge felt as if his own head was about to be pulled off.

"*Não sei,*" he pleaded.

"Oh, but you do know," said the detective, before letting go and stepping away.

Jorge plunged his head into his hands and began to cry uncontrollably. Between sobs, he repeated, aggrieved:

"In the name of *tudo quanto é santo,* I swear I know *nada... Pelo amor de Deus,* I know *nada...*"

8   *Parallel Investigation*

The thick auburn beard that framed Marcelo Braga's oval face gave him something of a Nordic look, while deep-set eyes suggested sleepless nights. Journalism had a hold on him as strong as did football. Although he was forever bad-mouthing the newspaper's owner and complaining about his salary, he loved his job. He felt like a fish in an aquarium when he was sitting in his editor's office, the faces of reporters and columnists, layout artists and illustrators, photographers and sub-editors looking in.

Whenever big stories broke – the fall of government *ministros*, currency crashes, bankruptcies, deaths of actors and celebrities – he would work for two or three days solid, surviving on ham sandwiches, coffee and cigarettes. As an editor, he satisfied his love of devising headlines, starting campaigns, making texts concise and presenting stories with maximum impact. But whenever he could, he returned to reporting.

Marcelo went for a drink every day after work, retiring to whichever *boteco* was the latest watering hole of choice among hacks. There he'd deliver alcohol-fuelled rants about chairmen, managers and the state of sports writing. He'd conjure up the names of players, form teams and predict results, genuinely convinced that nobody knew as much about football as he did.

A chronic Flamengo fan, he constantly engaged in banter with Jorge at the hotel. He also argued regularly with Diamante Negro, voices raised increasingly loud. Marcelo spoke in a shout, finding endless new energy from somewhere.

DUEL

Marcelo showed no sign of being intimidated as he sat before the detective. He was a whirlwind of anxiety on the inside, but not a single muscle betrayed this on the outside. The only outward sign of nerves was the short amount of time that elapsed between his putting one cigarette out and lighting another.

"What can you tell me about Seu Marçal's murder?" asked Del Bosco. The detective was acutely aware that he was dealing with a member of the press and had to handle the questioning with care. It was like a game of chess, with the need to anticipate your opponent's next move.

"Actually, I'd like you to tell me what the police have confirmed so far," replied Marcelo. The journalist subscribed to the view that the best form of defence was attack.

"We've uncovered several important clues," the detective bluffed.

Del Bosco was adept at getting the measure of the people he questioned. He knew some journalists weren't in the habit of distinguishing between what was said in private and what was divulged in public, and so he added, before Marcelo had a chance to ask:

"Clues that must, for the moment, remain undisclosed."

Marcelo drew hard on his cigarette.

"If the killer lived in the hotel, there's no way I wouldn't be able to spot him. It can't have been an inside job," he said, without a great deal of conviction.

Del Bosco leaned in over the table.

"It was an outside job, but with the assistance of someone on the inside. Nothing was broken into, no door was forced open. The killer came and went just like one of the residents."

"That's what intrigues me, too," said Marcelo, relaxing his guard. "How did someone break in and go on the rampage without any of us hearing so much as a sound, struggle or scream? But we've got it covered at the newspaper."

The last sentence sounded to Del Bosco like an insult and a challenge. Blood rose to his temples, as if to a wound to his professional pride. If the press solved the mystery before the police did, discredit and career demotion would come down on Del Bosco like a ton of bricks.

"I saw the story," said the detective, with visible restraint. "It speculated that Seu Marçal was murdered by someone with free transit about the hotel." He stared Marcelo in the eye and added, "Which would include you among the suspects…"

The detective's tone was mocking. He had been trying to prevent his feelings from boiling over, but now he rushed to press home his advantage and regain the initiative.

"Does your newspaper have access to some concrete clue, or is it pure conjecture?"

Marcelo didn't like what was being insinuated, but he chose not to object. He placed a new cigarette in his mouth, slowly moved his lighter up to it and took a deep, satisfied drag. He watched the spiral of smoke climb above the detective's head.

"The newspaper is conducting a parallel investigation," Marcelo said, as he exhaled a second drag. "And if you'll forgive me, Del Bosco, I haven't come here to give you an exclusive."

The detective stretched back in his chair, allowing his body to relax into a slump. He sketched out a smile and sighed.

"Investigation is the job of the police."

"*Ora*," began Marcelo defiantly, "unless you lot show a bit more urgency, we'll be the ones with the scoop, amigo."

"Are you saying you refuse to answer my questions?"

"Ask and I'll answer; I won't shirk my duties before the law," said Marcelo, conscious he'd been calling police authority into question. "But I'm not obliged to reveal my sources. Don't expect any revelations from me. I'm more inclined to help my newspaper."

MODERNIZATION

Being a member of a news team gave Marcelo more than just a sense of satisfaction. Having the power to promote or destroy people and institutions in a matter of two or three lines gave him confidence and security.

The press room was an extension of his self. He'd joined the profession shortly before entrance exams were introduced. New recruits had henceforth been required to brandish journalism degrees, an initiative that had significantly changed the profile of reporters. These days, clean-cut youngsters in fashionable suits dominated, IT experts who spoke a dialect that mixed Portuguese and English. They referred to New York as if they'd been born there and bowed in deference to every political and economic act of the post-industrial countries, while limiting criticism of their own government to a form of sarcasm that never risked challenging the elite's grip on power.

Marcelo lacked such subtleties. He stood out for his ability to transform any trivial fact into headline news, and yet he knew his style of journalism was becoming obsolete. Press rooms and editorial desks were modernizing and, just as monks no longer travelled the world saving souls, reporters no longer strayed from their desks. They had become acolytes of electronic paraphernalia. It was not unusual for them to implant their interpretation of the facts onto the facts themselves.

CLARIFICATION

"Could you at least clarify where you were at the time of Seu Marçal's murder?" said the detective.

"*Bem*, you saw me arrive at the hotel," Marcelo reminded him. "I got there just before the forensics. I was in Lamas, having a few beers with the guys from work, discussing the Brazil squad for the World Cup. If there's one thing that connects me to the crime, it's the fact that I was calling for the manager's head at the time of the murder. Oh, that someone might do to him what they did to Seu Marçal!"

9   *Shadows Offstage*

"Rosaura Dorotéia dos Santos," the girl said hesitantly. Delegado Del Bosco jotted her name down and tried to clear his head in preparation for the questioning.

Rosaura had short straight hair, moist eyes and a little dimple on her chin. Her appearance advertised her vanity: her hair was immaculately combed, her nails were painted salmon pink and her skin was saturated in creams. She'd grown up in Goiás, where she'd studied until second grade, but moved to Rio to pursue her dream of breaking into television. These days she was motivated by a singular obsession: to stop being a wage slave and become a *telenovela* star.

She collected variety magazines and decorated the walls of her room at the hotel with photos of actors and actresses. She spent hours in front of the mirror, playing the roles of imaginary characters, studying the expression in her eyes, the curve of her mouth, the posture of her shoulders, the gestures of her hands. Her mind was a stage on which she performed to herself, the sole spectator. She read and reread tales of television presenters who had been born in the interior, as she had. Girls from humble backgrounds who, through pluck and hard work, had overcome anonymity to reach the heights of success. But she became confused when she flicked through unauthorized biographies that told of TV stars who'd climbed the ladder of fame by acting in pornographic films, appearing naked in men's magazines and sleeping with media chiefs.

At weekends, she waited at the stage doors of television centres, elbowing her way through crowds of adolescents to fight for the privilege of sitting in the studio audience, the chance to watch her idols in action. As a female, she was almost always selected to bolster the contingent of *garotas* who stood and applauded before fainting spontaneously, as instructed on monitors the viewer at home couldn't see.

All the same, the best she'd managed in terms of an actual job was that of servant to a rich entrepreneur in a stately home. She took offence whenever people said she was a "domestic maid". She preferred to call herself a "precious-metals polishing specialist", an expression coined by Seu Marçal.

She was paid relatively well for the job. Every *centavo* she didn't spend on cosmetics, jewellery and clothes made by a neighbourhood seamstress, she set to one side, concerned as she was for her future. Nevertheless, she was certain her talent would one day be recognized by someone with influence, someone capable of putting her in front of the studio lights.

PREDICAMENT

"*Senhor*, I wouldn't hurt a fly," Rosaura said in an imploring and tearful tone, in response to the detective's insinuation that she might have had something to do with Seu Marçal's death.

"Rosaura, your situation is delicate to say the least." Del Bosco knew the best approach to interrogation varied according to the profile of the suspect, so he was being threatening, albeit somewhat reluctantly. "We have concrete information that you know who the killer is," he said, as per the *Manual*'s guidelines, under the chapter "Squeeze an Orange: Get Strawberry Juice".

The girl's cheeks went red. Then they turned pale. Floods of tears poured from her little round eyes. She took a hankie from her handbag and buried her face in it. Her shoulders rocked to the rhythm of her silent sobbing.

Del Bosco stood up, went over to her and ran his hand through her hair. The touch was pregnant with ambiguity, objectively purporting to be an act of comfort, subjectively showing the first stage of the male ready to pounce if the female opened the door.

"There's no need to cry," he said, stroking Rosaura's hair and restyling it with his fingers. "There's no actual evidence against you," he added, trying to supplant the image of authoritative police officer with that of affectionate and understanding gentleman, alive to her feminine charms.

Rosaura kept her head bowed, her body having tensed up at the unexpected and unwanted touch of the detective.

He went on, now inflecting his voice with a hint of the paternal:

"All I'm saying is that I've received certain information, information that may prove to be unfounded. All you have to do is tell me exactly what you know," he said, before taking a step back, "and then I'll send you on your way."

"*Senhor*, I've got nothing to do with the crime. I barely even used to say *tudo bom* to Seu Marçal."

"Do you suspect Diamante Negro?" asked the detective, swiftly switching from confrontation to complicity. "Could it not have been Professor Cândido? Or, who knows, maybe Marcelo?" He paused, before trying to exonerate himself:

"One of them mentioned your name, doubtless to divert our lines of inquiry. And what about Doutor Pacheco? Can you be sure it wasn't him?"

Rosaura noticed the portrait of the Presidente da República and felt uncomfortable. It looked like *o presidente* was staring at her.

"Diamante Negro is the way he is, but deep down he's a good person," said the girl. "Professor Cândido has his head full of books, but his heart is with the street kids. He's always considerate to me, though I don't think he even knows my name. Doutor Pacheco is a bit of a *safado*, always leching after my legs, but he's an important man. Why would he run the risk of ending up in jail if he dreams of becoming president? I don't like Marcelo. He talks too much and sticks his nose into things. But I don't think he's a killer because of it."

"And Jorge?"

"He's the only one like me at the hotel, *delegado*. He was born poor, struggles, causes nobody any harm. Quite the opposite: folk trample all over him and the poor *rapaz* never says a word."

"Do you suspect any of the women in the hotel?" asked Del Bosco, his lust having subsided.

"Dona Dinó is a saint; her head is in heaven more than it is on earth. I'd rather not talk about Madame Larência."

"Why not?" said Del Bosco. "Your silence might be interpreted as an accusation."

"I don't suspect her," said Rosaura, "I just don't have any sympathy for *cafetinas*. It's bad enough that menfolk exploit prostitutes, but a woman!"

"Where were you at the time of the murder?"

"In the shower. I'd just finished supper."

10   *The Cat and the Old Lady*

For her appearance at the police station, Dona Dinó had chosen a green full-skirted dress that gathered at the waist. She wore an alpaca hat atop her snowy-white hair, a hat that made her head too hot and that she found to be an uncomfortable accessory, one inappropriate to Rio's tropical climate. Nevertheless, she wore it, for the same reason other women submitted themselves to similar tortures: she believed the hat made her look more beautiful. She wielded one further accessory: the thick-coated Osíris, his eyes oscillating between the various features of the room.

"Does *senhora* have any idea, any evidence or clue, that might help our investigation?" asked Del Bosco, wondering why the old lady was wearing such a ridiculous hat.

"*Não*," she said with a tired, expressionless voice. "I sleep at the back of the hotel, *delegado*. I barely know what goes on in the guest wing. Especially at night."

"The killing took place between nine and ten o'clock," said the detective. "Does *senhora* really go to bed that early?"

"Around ten."

"And so where was *senhora* at the time of the murder?"

"In my room saying my evening prayers. The *novena de São Dionísio*. One of my patron saints."

"And *senhora* didn't hear any strange noises?"

The woman paused. She needed time to think.

"When I pray, I only have eyes and ears for heaven."

"How long has the house operated as a hotel?"

"It used to belong to Professor Hórus," Dona Dinó explained. "An Egyptian. He came to Brazil to research a plant the *índios* make tea out of to induce visions. I was his governess for many years. When he left the country, he asked me to take charge of the property. I didn't have the resources to pay for its upkeep. I had to turn it into a hotel."

"What can *senhora* tell me about Diamante Negro?"

Dona Dinó plunged her hands into Osíris's fur, nervously running her fingers along his back and up to his tail.

"He's the embodiment of a fallen angel. He has the looks of a man and the ways of a woman. He was friendly with Seu Marçal. The night it happened, he was out working the streets."

"Could Doutor Pacheco be the killer?" said Del Bosco impatiently.

Dona Dinó hesitated.

"The *doutor* is a man of many obsessions. He speaks in a way my head can't compute. He'd do well not to be so conceited. He lives his life hanging around with bigwigs. But he has a good heart. Why would he kill Seu Marçal? He's too soft to have committed such an outrage."

Dona Dinó spoke leaning forward over the cat, the tip of a finger poking up the brim of her hat. Del Bosco put his knees up against the table edge and rocked back on his chair, his weight on its hind legs.

"Dona Dinó, wouldn't the caretaker have cause to hate the victim?"

"Jorge!?" she exclaimed in surprise, curling her lips into a subtle smile. "He doesn't even kill the cockroaches infesting his room. Besides, if he were a killer, he wouldn't have to chop anyone's head off. The *rapaz* could just poison the food."

"Tell me about Madame Larência?"

"Her spirit is conflicted. Her *orixás* don't match. She still needs to pass through several incarnations. But she was very fond of Seu Marçal. She sold gemstones for him."

The detective put the front legs of his chair back on the floor and leaned over the table to stare at Dona Dinó from close quarters.

"Couldn't she have double-crossed him?" he said in a low, firm tone. "Couldn't she have racked up debts with him? Couldn't she have contracted someone to kill him?"

Dona Dinó drew comfort from a cuddle with the cat.

"I don't know anything about their business dealings. But they got on well. I even thought they'd make a good couple. But she seemed only to have eyes for his gemstones."

Del Bosco stood up to exercise his legs and his impatience, then suggested:

"I think we're on to something. Seu Marçal and Madame Larência were lovers. He couldn't keep his eyes off other women and so she killed him out of jealousy!"

"*Senhor*, Larência is not the sort of woman to be jealous of anyone. She's a lady of the night. Unless she were in love. A woman's love is blind."

"Tell me about the other guests."

Dona Dinó arranged the cat about her neck.

"Professor Cândido is the most educated of them all. He must have been a prince in a previous life. Or a mountain hermit. He studied to become a priest, so he's well trained. He looks after abandoned street children. He'd never do a thing like this. Marcelo is a bit of a loose cannon. He likes attention. But he was friendly with Seu Marçal. He works for the newspaper. He wasn't home at the time of the incident."

Del Bosco interrupted her, irritated:

"Dona Dinó, don't be so naive. It might seem as though whoever killed Seu Marçal wasn't home at the time, but we don't know that until we identify the killer. Someone was in his room, that's for sure."

"Rosaura is a fool," Dona Dinó went on unmoved, her fingers combing Osíris's hair. "Aside from going to work, the *menina* spends her whole time daydreaming of becoming a *telenovela* actress."

II

THE COLLECTION

1   *The Proposal*

Cândido put the phone down, feeling confused and intrigued. He hadn't entirely understood what Eduardo Lassale was proposing: something to do with an editorial project. It was hard enough to understand the publisher face to face, let alone over the phone. Lassale was as incoherent as he was ambitious.

Lassale had inherited a small *livraria* from his father. Besides books, the shop had sold stationery, which enabled it to survive in times of crisis. Aldo Lassale, a stout Italian with a round face and fat fingers, had come to Brazil fleeing the war. After first working as a translator of operas and plays, he'd opened the *livraria*, without knowing that Brazilians had neither the custom nor resources to consume books like the Europeans.

The *Divina Comédia* had occupied a white corner building in Tijuca, with wide doors leading onto both streets. When first opened, the shop had stocked only classics, but space on the shelves was soon found for popular fiction, serials and almanacs. A magazine section came next, and before long half the shop was given over to exercise books, notepads and pens.

Aldo Lassale passed on to his son a firm belief that Brazilians did in fact read, indeed they read a lot; they just didn't read books, because books were expensive and, as a general rule, written in a language that was inaccessible to most of the population. Brazilians read adverts, leaflets, calendars, newspapers and magazines, anything that used simple, straightforward vocabulary. There was a huge untapped market for the publisher who managed to find a way of exploiting such reading habits by providing books that were accessible to the public at large.

Eduardo grew up believing his mission in life was to realize his father's dream. When old Aldo died of pneumonia – provoked, according to the doctors, by the mould on his collection of antique works, which he insisted on leafing through every night before bed – his son sold the *livraria* and used the money to buy a property on Alto da Boa Vista, where he founded Editora Hellas. The building was a two-storey house with a garden. It had a veranda extension that served as the publisher's entrance hall and held a display of recent publications.

INTRUSIVE

Cândido's uncertainty may have had something to do with the old lady staring at him from the other side of the room. Dona Dinó, dressed in espadrilles and a faded brown-and-white checked dress, sat watching him as he used the phone, her hands gripped to the red handle of her broom. Her affection for him was evident in the warmth of her eyes. It certainly wasn't obvious in her speech: she was a woman of few words and short sentences; minimal punctuation and much reticence. But although she wrapped herself in silence, the force of her inquisitive eyes gave her a strange magnetism.

INTERLUDE

"Did he not explain himself properly, or is it my head that's fuzzy?"

"No, you're right, man," Odidnac reassured him. "He was over-excited."

THE INTERRUPTED SHOWER

The phone call had been an offer of work. Most likely another of the publisher's hare-brained schemes, but it was hard to tell: Lassale's enthusiasm had been such that he'd failed to get the message over. He suffered from a stammer and had trouble expressing himself when he got excited. His thoughts seemed to sprout wings and take off, but when it came to articulating them, they came out like the plodding steps of a rheumatic dancing to a *samba batucada*.

Nevertheless, he'd sold a million copies of *How to be Happy in Times of Crisis* by Ricardo Kost, and *The Handbook of Conjugal Survival* by Ciça and Zezito Alves – partners on and off the page – was on its thirty-eighth edition. *Hug a Tree and Feel Happy* by Tiago Camporubro was the latest title flying off the shelves and filling the publisher's coffers.

PRESENTIMENT

Cândido was feeling crabby, and not because of the old lady's indiscreet snooping or the way her eyes questioned him. It was because he'd been in the shower when she'd called him to the phone and he hated having his morning routine interrupted.

He'd been standing under the water with his eyes closed and his mouth open, shampoo rinsing from his hair, naked-ness freeing his head of all thought and leading him towards the imperceptible, when he'd heard a dry tap-tap at the door.

He could tell it was Dona Dinó from the deadness of the sound: she always used the handle of her broom to knock at the door.

Cândido hated being hurried. He liked doing everything in his own time. The unexpected flustered him.

CAREFUL

Yet Cândido really couldn't complain about Dona Dinó. She treated him like the son she'd never had, always worrying over the fact that he ate so little, studied so much and spent all his spare time trying to help young delinquents. He ran himself into the ground, she said, so much so that he often mistook the salt cellar for the sugar shaker.

THE ARRIVAL

Cândido had been living in Rio for several months. He'd arrived one sunny, humid morning after a long and tiring bus journey. The descent through the Serra das Araras, with the road twisting down mountain slopes, had upset his stomach. His queasiness was not helped by the foul smell of rotten water he encountered on Avenida Brasil. On first impression, he thought with some disappointment, there was nothing very *maravilhosa* about the so-called Marvellous City. There was rubbish piled up at the roadside, *barraco* shacks behind garages and warehouses, fire and smoke pouring out of the chimneys of the Duque de Caxias refinery, buses flying along at breakneck speed – everything was dirty and noisy compared to the town he'd left behind.

He got off the bus at the *rodoviária*, thinking he'd entered Rio de Janeiro by the back door. A human ant trail filed in with the spluttering motorcade of buses, exhaust fumes clogging the platforms with carbon gases; the information desk was closed, the toilets stank of urine. Taxi drivers fought over fares with a ferocity that spoke of ill intentions.

It was only much later that Cândido discovered that, despite the filth and poverty, Rio was an enchanting city, with a beauty to delight the eyes and revitalize the spirit.

On arriving at Hotel Brasil, he was examined from head to toe by Dona Dinó's lynxlike eyes. The old lady looked into the depths of his soul and scrutinized his slim, beardless face, his broad forehead, his straight fringe and his hazelnut eyes – eyes that held a certain sadness.

His white shirt was soaked with sweat. He carried minimal luggage: one small holdall containing a few clothes, basic toiletries and a copy of *The Cloud of Unknowing*, the work of an anonymous fourteenth-century Englishman.

THE FATAL BLOW

A week earlier, Cândido's fiancée had told him she was in love with another man. His face had frozen in fury. He'd held her and shaken her, as if trying to dislodge the errant feeling. All he'd managed was to make her cry, an uncontrollable bout of

93

sobbing, as if she were cleansing her soul ready to welcome in her new love. Cândido secretly admired her courage. If it had been the other way round, he'd never have dared upset her so. But she was a woman, he told himself. Women didn't do things by halves.

He'd always thought love at first sight only happened in novels and films. He was deeply hurt. He became fragile, blinded by the swirl of emotions. He felt his soul dry out, jealousy seep through his pores, humiliation shatter his self-esteem; his steps became hesitant, his head was unable to complete thoughts, sadness suffocated him.

It wasn't a physical pain, localized, something the spirit might defend itself against or reason relieve. His spirit had crumbled and been swallowed up by a vast chasm. He loved Ângela, who loved another man. He took up an ascetic lifestyle, the crazed martyrdom of the estranged.

He realized his suffering was too big for the small Minas town where he lived, a town that obliged him to be too close to Ângela's joyful heart when his own heart was in pieces.

He decided to leave.

RECEPTION

That first day in Rio, he'd wandered about the city-centre streets for several hours, choking on the heat coming off the tarmac. Then a mansion on Largo da Lapa caught his eye: Hotel Brasil. It was a grey building in neoclassical French style, sombre-looking and dilapidated, but shaded by exuberant *mangueiras*.

The entrance stood at the top of a rotting wooden staircase with a handrail ravaged by termites. A rusty old sign read: "Rooms for single ladies and gentlemen. Family environment."

The landlady led him into a parlour, which was desperately dark compared to the outside light that still reverberated in his eyes. Dona Dinó weighed up his moral stature and placed Osíris at his feet. The cat opened and closed its glowing eyes and licked its front right paw.

The landlady stressed that the hotel was a *hotel residencial*, then handed him a guest form and asked him where he was from.

Cândido told her he'd been born and raised in Minas Gerais, then become a novice in a monastery in the Mantiqueira mountains. After giving up the frock, he'd taught Portuguese in a rural school.

"I consider it divine providence," exclaimed Dona Dinó, "to welcome into my house a guest of such distinguished background." She was a pious woman, though her church was broad and she lit candles to an assorted assembly of gods and saints: she made *umbanda* offerings at crossroads, visited *candomblé* temples, attended séances, drank indigenous potions, observed horoscopes and cowrie-shell divinations, and followed Egyptian esotericism and Indian asceticism, all with equal conviction.

THE HEIRESS

A poor girl from the *favelas*, Dinó first got a job as a cleaner in the house she'd go on to govern, then turn into the rather grandly named Hotel Brasil. When she'd started out, the owner of the house had been Hórus, an Egyptian. A devotee of Thor, he taught his young maid to worship the natural world and introduced her to the spirits of the Nile and Ganges. He would often spend months in the Amazon, fascinated by indigenous beliefs, river legends and forest myths. While he was away, he would entrust his mansion to Dinó, the only disciple he ever raised in Brazil.

One day, overcome with supernatural inspiration, Hórus took down the hammer that adorned his study wall and made to leave without explanation. He bid Dinó farewell, telling her to take care of the house and giving her a present she was to look after "with the same affection the Madonna showed Jesus". That present was Osíris, the cat with the golden eyes.

MOVING

Dona Dinó was only too pleased to have Cândido in the hotel, though she thought it sad that God had not seen fit to find for the former novice a good woman. Nevertheless, she made sure to repeat her customary warnings: rent must never be in arrears; no visitors allowed in any of the rooms; never touch her broom or feed the cat.

Three days later, a removal van pulled up outside the hotel with a few personal belongings and two big boxes of books.

Dona Dinó convinced herself she was housing a genius. Perhaps Cândido was even as far advanced along the spiritual path as Hórus had been.

THE PHONE CALL

Landlady and tenant kept a healthy distance in front of the other guests, though if anything this strengthened the bond between them. She even broke one of her golden rules for him, excusing him his rent when he was out of work. And she allowed him to use the phone. She did so to aid his voluntary work with street kids, but, regardless, it was an exceptional privilege: the other guests were only allowed to receive calls; to make calls, they had to go out and use the phone booth in the street. For incoming calls, Dona Dinó hurried along to the guest's room and tapped at the door with the tip of her broom, taking messages with undisguised displeasure if the guest happened to be out.

She tapped harder than usual that morning: the voice on the other end of the line sounded imploring, as if desperate for help. She hammered away with her broom handle, trying to make herself heard over the noise of the shower.

Cândido shouted for her to wait a moment – "I heard you, I'm coming" – feeling harassed and fighting a strange urge to go out into the corridor nude, as if it really was that urgent, as if someone was calling to tell him the end of the world was nigh and they had two days to live.

He turned the tap on full blast, rinsed, turned the water off, dried and put his dressing gown on inside out, all with the haste of someone who hated making people wait. When he got to the dining room he found Dona Dinó sitting on the window sill, holding her broom and waiting patiently to listen in on the conversation, showing no scruples about it.

Cândido held the phone away from his ear: Lassale was shouting as if he were calling from the top floor of a burning building. The publisher was garbling his words. Syllables raced off his tongue but tripped over his lips, making everything come out disjointed.

Unsure whether the problem was the way the editor was talking or how he was listening, Cândido cut his losses and said he'd drop by the publisher's to discuss things.

SCRUPULOUS FORGER

Given the intellectual training he'd received, first at the monastery and later as a teacher, Cândido passed the Hellas entrance exam with little difficulty.

"What is it you want me to do?" he asked Lassale, on being admitted into the fold.

"I want you to rewrite books," said the editor. "Many authors have talent in terms of ideas and style, but border on the illiterate when it comes to spelling and grammar. They mix tenses, repeat words, use multiple adjectives, confuse agreements and endings – they basically can't get their ideas down properly. I want you to go over badly drafted texts and turn them into something our readers can digest and comprehend."

TASKS

Tucked away in his room in Hotel Brasil, surrounded by the empty orange boxes he'd turned into bookcases, Cândido rewrote texts with the scrupulous care of a forger. Between tasks, he headed over to the Casa do Menor in Baixada Fluminense, where he read the children stories and helped them learn to read and write.

THIRD MILLENNIUM

It was late morning by the time Cândido pulled up outside Hellas on his motorbike. He found Lassale in high spirits. The publisher looked like a lord in his study, hemmed in behind a wall of books. When Cândido sat down opposite him, they could barely see one another through the pile of manuscripts on the desk.

"In this country," said Lassale, as he cleared away some of the clutter, "there are more writers than readers!"

He calmed down when his comment received no response.

"How's the murder investigation going at the hotel?"

"It looks like they're back where they started," said Cândido. "They question us over and over again, the forensics re-examine the scene of the crime and the Lapa *delegado* assures us he'll lay hands on the killer any day now. But I don't believe him."

"Do you suspect anyone?"

"Seu Marçal was a strange guy," said Cândido. "He was from the sticks like me, but he loved the big city. He wasn't uneducated, but he didn't show a great deal of understanding about anything, either. I think he liked living on the edge. There must have been some kind of funny business lurking behind those gemstones."

"A mafia hit?" the editor suggested, quickly adding: "It would make a good book."

"There's no doubt he was killed by professionals," said Cândido. "You can't commit an atrocity like that and leave no clues unless you know what you're doing."

"Could it have been anyone at the hotel?" said Lassale.

"I doubt it. But I wouldn't rule out one of the guests being an accomplice and having let the killer in."

"Like who?" asked Lassale, putting his papers down and laying his hands on the desk.

"I'd rather not name names; I don't want to be accused of being an unreliable witness," Cândido backtracked. He changed the subject: "What was it you wanted to see me about?"

"I want you to take on a new job," said the editor, as if handing out a prize. He spoke slowly and precisely, choosing his words with care. "A new century is underway, with society facing a crisis of depression, social and sexual role reversal and mass unemployment due to technological evolution. At the same time, we're seeing a return of subjectivity and a yearning for spirituality. I want to respond to these concerns and demands by launching a new collection for the third millennium: *Terceiro Milênio*. We'll provide readers with a scientific, historical, philosophical – even a religious – perspective on this whole postmodern business of values being relative, traditions disappearing, taboos breaking, generosity disappearing. We'll publish the collection as serials and I want you to write them up, offering the public insight into its main anxieties. What do you say?"

Cândido felt cheated. He liked rewriting other people's texts. Producing his own material didn't appeal to him at all. Especially when his own literary tastes bore no comparison to Lassale's.

INTERLUDE

"Odid, Lassale has more interest in the market than he does in talent, wouldn't you say?"

"Come on, man, why go criticizing the boss?" said Odidnac. "He's a businessman. Like all businessmen, the first thing he looks for is financial return."

"He could at least do so with slightly less vulgar publications," sighed Cândido.

"Don't be so naive. He does whatever offers good profit margins."

PLACEBO

"I think my opinion probably counts for little," said Cândido, sounding disappointed. "I can tell you're enthusiastic about the idea, so the best thing for me to do is just embrace it. I assume this won't mean a doubling of my workload?"

"Of course not!" said Lassale, with little conviction. "Consider yourself relieved from correcting texts. Now you create them."

"My only hope," sighed Cândido, "is that I can come up with something that amounts to more than a mere literary placebo."

Lassale picked up on the subtext. The editor leaned forward in his chair and put his elbows on the desk. He interlocked the fingers of his hands underneath his jaw and leaned his chin on his thumbs. He made an effort to contain his excitement, the better to control the rhythm of his speech and thoughts.

"The literary placebo is as effective as the medicinal one," he said, battling a slight stammer. "It may not act upon the social organism itself, but it does have a positive collateral impact. It broadens people's outlook, provides oxygen for the spirit, soothes the soul, rids sinners of guilt, spreads belief that a world without conflict is possible and – not the least of it – creates a new readership and familiarizes them with the act of reading."

Lassale paused, as if choosing which metaphor to pluck from the sky.

"It's like breathing in incense: the pleasant odour stimulates our sense of smell for as long as there's smoke in the air. I'm not a missionary, nor do I harbour any intention of founding a church. I just want to publish texts that allow people to forget their worries for a while. Give them a semantic lift, make them feel better, more connected to their beliefs."

The editor was getting carried away, a maelstrom of ideas swirling around beneath his thick grey hair. Cândido tried to bring him back down to earth.

"I don't find the opportunity to go scrambling about physical and spiritual nooks and crannies particularly appealing."

"You'll be swapping retail for wholesale," said Lassale, paying no attention. "Do you know Doutor Bramante and Doutora Kundali?" It was clearly a question designed to provoke a reaction rather than an answer.

Cândido knew nobody. He barely knew the name of the Presidente da República, though he was well versed in the vernacular of government, having read thick treaties written in the language of office. He saw himself as a hillbilly booklover whose parachute had, by chance, landed in the big city.

"Roberval Bramante is a leading sexologist," said Lassale, "and Mônica Kundali an acclaimed anthropologist. Like many stars of the science constellation, their names are not known to the wider public; they prefer the fluorescent lights of research labs to the studio lights of television sets. Together with them, you'll form the triumvirate responsible for the collection."

Cândido's face showed absolute indifference. The editor stood up to bid him farewell.

"We're having dinner with Bramante tomorrow night," Lassale said as he walked Cândido to the door. "The *doutora* had a prior engagement, but you'll meet her next week."

Lassale called out to Cândido as he left:

"Careful now! Don't go getting your head chopped off – I need it!"

FRACAS

A scream of terror cut through the early morning, waking Cândido from his dreamy sleep. The sound of shattering glass made him bristle with fear. He got out of bed, put on his white dressing gown and slowly opened the door. He saw Pacheco standing in the corridor in his breeches, his body scratched and bleeding.

"Help! Pervert! *Filho de uma vaca!*" yelled Rosaura from inside her room. "Poliiiiice!"

Pacheco was pleading with her to open the door, to let him explain.

Diamante Negro, wrapped in a red Chinese crêpe kimono, poked his head out into the corridor.

"What's going on? Has *sua excelência* taken to raping *garotas* now?"

"Shut up, everyone!" hollered Madame Larência from behind her door. "I need my beauty sleep!"

Jorge arrived on the scene, wielding his fish knife.

"I went to the dining room to get a glass of water," said Pacheco, imploringly, "but I didn't take my glasses, and on the way back I got the wrong door. It was dark. I accidentally went into Rosaura's room. I only realized my mistake when she screamed and threw something at me."

"What drivel, Pacheco, what utter drivel," said Marcelo, coming out of his room in a blue dressing gown. "Admit it: you thought tart was on the menu and ended up with humble pie."

"Open the door, Rosaura!" Jorge insisted. "Dona Dinó wants to talk to you. In the dining room."

He turned to Pacheco.

"And the *doutor*, too."

The landlady was sitting at the head of the table, holding her broom like a staff. Osíris clung to her with his eyes closed, moulded to her bosom.

Diamante Negro got some cotton wool from the first-aid box and started cleaning Pacheco's wounds. The political aide felt rather self-conscious standing there half naked. He kept his head down, as if fascinated by the daisies in the pattern of the tablecloth. His lack of spectacles gave his appearance a particular ridiculousness.

Rosaura entered the room in a salmon-coloured nightdress, crying against Jorge's shoulder.

"What happened, Rosaura?" asked Dona Dinó.

"This is all one big misunderstanding!" said Pacheco, before turning to Diamante Negro. "Owwwww!"

"Keep still, *criatura*. I'm not going to castrate you. It's just a splash of iodine – to stop the cut from becoming as infected as your mind!"

"I wasn't asking *senhor*," stressed Dona Dinó. "I asked the girl."

"Speak up, *menina*," said Jorge, by Rosaura's side.

"He," she said in a trembling voice, pointing a finger at Pacheco, "came into my room and tried to get into my bed."

"It was a mistake," Pacheco repeated.

"There's no smoke without fire," said Dona Dinó. "Come on, let's have the whole story, *garota*."

"He promised to get me a place in the chorus line of a TV show. I suppose he thought he'd cash the favour in early, before it had even been fulfilled. So I smashed the lamp over his head."

"And what does the *doutor* have to say for himself?" asked Dona Dinó.

"It's true, I did promise to help her. But I never asked for anything in return. I'm a man of principles. What happened tonight was that I simply got the wrong door – our rooms are side by side."

"Shock! Horror! Pacheco is a liar and a philanderer!" said Marcelo, who'd come in and sat down opposite Dona Dinó.

The landlady gave them all a lecture on morals and how she expected them to behave. Then she dismissed the guests, though not without a warning.

"If this happens again, you'll be out on the street – both of you."

Dona Dinó stood up, sending Osíris sliding down her legs. The cat landed on its feet, marched across the room, back held high, and settled down by the stove.

2   *Dinner*

Lassale had booked a table at one of the most traditional restaurants in town. It was housed in a former market hall shaped like a giant birdcage, at the boat terminal on Praça XV. Green wooden shutters opened onto a view of Guanabara bay, Pão de Açúcar standing out against the sea in the background, bursting out of the silvery waters into the bright moonlight.

Cândido walked in and found himself lost among a sea of waiters and diners. He scanned the room for Lassale but couldn't find him. He set off in search. As he walked between tables and chairs, he tried not to look at people's plates: he considered eating to be deserving of privacy, even when done in public. Just looking at the diners felt intrusive, but he had no choice if he was to find the publisher.

He eventually spotted Lassale at a candlelit table by the window out the back, in the company of another man.

Roberval Bramante was holding a small curved pipe flat against his chin. His eyes had a dull shine, his nose was hooked like a bell and he was stoutly built. His long curly hair, streaked with the first signs of grey, fell down to his shoulders.

Lassale welcomed Cândido in an effusive fashion and Bramante stood up with some difficulty to greet him. He seemed reserved, as if instinctively suspicious of newcomers.

"So here's our scribbler," said Lassale, as the attentive *maître* appeared at Cândido's side and handed him a menu. Cândido laid a napkin on his knee and settled himself. Lassale proposed that they all have shrimp and selected *camarões à grega* for himself. The scientist followed suit and chose *camarões à baiana*.

Cândido had never had shrimp before and couldn't tell the difference between all the different options. In the end he chose *camarões fritos*, thinking that fried promised fewest surprises. Lassale ordered a nice bottle of *vinho branco* to go with it.

The *doutor* cleared his throat and gently tapped the bowl of his pipe against the edge of the ashtray. He rearranged himself in his chair, lit his pipe and motioned for Lassale to carry on the conversation they'd been having before Cândido arrived.

They'd been talking about sexuality.

"I was only saying that while you can point it out, you can never cancel it out," Lassale said cautiously, fearing the scientist might refute his layman's claim and realize that, although he was the publisher, he was much less cultured than he liked to make out.

"It's the same as the impulse to breathe or to eat. At birth, our first instinct is to seek the maternal breast. Pure fulfilment!" said Bramante. He released a puff of smoke right into Cândido's face, leaving him with no choice but to inhale the syrupy fumes. The scientist went on, a strange smile sketching itself on his face. "Babies manage to harmonize three basic pleasures: breathing, feeding and sucking at breasts. It's no simple thing: you try drinking a whole bottle of water without taking your mouth off the bottle! I'll show you – watch!"

He drew a waiter over, who was laden down with a tray of dirty plates from the next table.

"Hey, amigo," he said, holding out a bottle of mineral water, "if you can drink this bottle in one, you'll earn a good tip."

INTERLUDE

"Odid, this guy's so full of himself!"

"Calm down, man, give him a chance. Can't you see he's just trying to impress the boss?"

"But I worry he's going to be a nightmare to work with."

"You worry about your own work," said Odidnac. "Do too many cartwheels and you'll fall flat on your ass."

WONDER

The waiter paused. He needed a moment to process what he'd heard.

"Whenever I get thirsty, *senhor*, I go and have a glass of water in there," he said, pointing to the kitchen door with his chin.

The waiter went on his way. Bramante put the bottle back on the table.

Cândido broke the awkward silence.

"The more we try and rationalize what comes naturally to a baby, the more we run into trouble. Can we not see sexuality as something more than a merely reproductive or sensory act?"

Bramante rolled his eyes to the ceiling and exhaled a puff of smoke. Sensing a chance to test Cândido, he turned to him and said:

"Is that the way you see it?"

Cândido felt pressurized. He didn't want to start an argument with his new colleague.

"I often wonder," he said, feeling self-conscious, "how we might recover the liturgical aspect sexuality had in primitive times. For the more spiritually inclined Orientals, the pleasure lies not so much in the orgasm as in the communion of bodies and the effusion of the spirit. We Westerners are a long way from understanding such wonder."

Bramante smiled, though Cândido couldn't tell whether out of empathy or mockery. It seemed the *doutor* was about to say something, but he was interrupted by the *maître*.

FAROFA

The *maître* had come to take their knives and forks away. Cândido tried to hold on to his.

"What am I supposed to eat with?" he said in a loud voice.

"I'll bring *senhor* the appropriate cutlery," the *maître* whispered in his ear, before bowing like a pianist grateful for applause.

When the new cutlery arrived, Cândido studied it suspiciously, thinking such a tiny knife and fork could only be appropriate for dessert.

Bramante was absorbed with his own thoughts and seemed not to have noticed any of this. Cândido wanted to ask him if the baby sucked for the pleasure of the milk or the breast. He resisted so as not to come across as prosaic. Right then he felt more inclined to the first hypothesis: he was starving and wouldn't swap his meal for any woman in the world.

Nevertheless, he felt apprehensive. He would have preferred to be about to tuck into a *feijão tropeiro* or chicken and *farofa*. He loved *farofa*! He loved it whether it was made out of manioc flour, bread flour or maize, whether it was fried in butter or egg yolk, whether it was mixed with olives, raisins or banana. He hadn't tried shrimp before – it was quite a rarity in Minas – but he'd heard that, besides being expensive, it was very tasty.

"Centuries of repression," said the *doutor*, "have bequeathed us a schizophrenia whereby we flick between affection and sex. One day we'll free ourselves of our taboos and repression and become sexually unitarian again. We'll return to our original state of innocence – even incest will no longer be anathema."

"The primordial freedom experienced by Adam and Eve," suggested Cândido.

"Experienced and lost," said Lassale.

Bramante gave them both a stern look. His face seemed to swell. His voice came out somehow deeper.

"Forgive me, but it wasn't lost because of sex. God, if he exists, clearly won't tolerate competitors. That the forbidden fruit was Adam and Eve's desire for one another is a nonsense priests feed the gullible. That may be forbidden territory to the priests, but it wasn't to Adam and Eve, and if they hadn't screwed, we wouldn't be here talking about it. As far as sex was concerned, the first couple was free to do exactly as they pleased."

"And without the risk of being unfaithful," said Lassale, laughing at his own observation.

Bramante became excited, hoping he might shock Cândido.

"Exactly! Adam and Eve were mere reproductive moulds who got ideas above their station and started naming the livestock, a divine prerogative in a world yet to discover science. That's why they were punished."

110

The scientist picked up his wine and took a sip. Cândido made the most of the pause.

"Adam and Eve are the paradigms; God is the mystery that excites our curiosity," he said, as if the monk inside him had awoken from its slumber.

Bramante interrupted him.

"It's impossible to draw definitive conclusions about anything, much less find proper answers, without research. The primordial couple's problem was that they trusted too much in instinct. They were banging their heads against a brick wall!"

Before the conversation could confuse Cândido any further, the food arrived. The shrimp were large and pink, though Cândido thought them ugly and his portion small.

INTERLUDE

"Odid, they could at least have taken the eyes out! How did they survive the frying? Although on second thoughts, maybe it's better this way, so as not to remind me of Seu Marçal's head!"

"But still, you'd think they'd remove the heads – remember what Diamante Negro said to Pacheco?"

"And how are you supposed to eat the thing?"

"I don't know, man, but if you've been given kids' cutlery, I guess they must be pretty soft."

THE FLIGHT

Cândido put a shrimp in his mouth and bit into it.

"Ow! It's rock hard! It's like eating fried plastic."

"Take the shell off," said Lassale.

Cândido speared the fork into the shrimp's neck and picked up the knife with the curved end. He prodded it into the *camarão*, trying to force it open, but the thing slipped, slid across his greasy plate, flew across the table and landed in Lassale's lap. The publisher stood up, somewhat aggrieved, and called for a waiter.

The *maître* came rushing over and sent someone to fetch hot water. He made a compress out of a napkin and applied it to the stain, then poured salt on top to absorb the fat.

"It's best to use your fingers," said Bramante.

Cândido apologized and took Bramante's advice. He soon confirmed the disappointing truth: there was more crust on the crustacean than there was meat. He'd have much preferred a good pan-fried steak.

Not wanting to remain the centre of attention, Cândido asked the sexologist to go on with what he'd been saying.

Bramante turned to Lassale and talked as he chewed.

"I love the idea. A collection of periodicals for the masses!" He gave a self-satisfied sigh, wafting a hand in the air. "I can picture it on news stands now! We'll shine a light on all manner of sexual behaviour, from venereal disease to the morally perverse and the pathologically deviant." He brought his hand down and placed it on the publisher's arm, before continuing enthusiastically: "We'll broach pornography, Eros, Philia and Agape; Dharma, Artha and Kama; the Encratites and Don Juanism."

"And eroticism in art and worship," added Cândido.

INTERLUDE

"If old Gordo could only see me now, Odid, in high-minded rumination on the most base parts of the human organism."

"Doubtless the good abbot would say, 'the profanity of science leads the soul to the flames.'"

INCOMPATIBILITIES

Cândido liked to spend his spare time reading books, but the abbot, concerned about the upkeep of the monastery, didn't like him being in the library.

"Come join the community in caring for the cows and sheep, cultivating the vegetable patch, making things in the workshop. A novice's hands should always be either up or down: raised in oration or plunged into the soil. I will not have you sitting here for hours on end with your head buried in books."

All the same, Cândido became a compulsive reader at the monastery. He felt at home among the mahogany bookcases, the shelves packed with tantalizing spines and arranged into themes: theology, mysticism, philosophy, literature… He learned to read by topic rather than by book, except when reading a novel. He'd select a collection of books that broached the subject that interested him, pile them up on a table by the window and work his way through them, finding what was relevant by consulting the indices. He made notes on sheets of paper, writing in a tiny, slightly childish hand.

THE BOWL

The waiter placed a small silver bowl beside Cândido. Wrapped in a napkin, it contained steaming water and had a slice of lemon stuck to the rim. He thought it strange that the other diners had not been afforded the same consideration. Perhaps it was an accompaniment to the dish he'd ordered.

INTERLUDE

"Odid, this guy is a pervert."

"Calm down, man! He's an expert in his field."

"Any idea what this bowl is for?"

"I think it contains a special tea for digesting whatever it was you ordered."

CONNECTIONS

Lassale helped himself to another glass of *vinho*, preferring not to respond to the *doutor*'s enthusiasm. As a publisher, he was used to dealing with a wide range of authors with a wide range of beliefs. He tried to prevent any personal issues from arising by keeping his counsel at table.

Cândido finally made up his mind: he squeezed the lemon into the water, picked the bowl up with both hands and drank. Before he could take a second sip, the scientist had hold of his arm.

"That's not for drinking," he said, "it's for washing the grease off your fingers."

Cândido thanked him, blushing with shame. Bramante went back to the laborious task of relighting his pipe. Lassale gave a deep sigh, trying to stop a yawn.

"So, in summary, I suggest the two of you work together to explain the connections between sexuality and spirituality."

114

"Is *senhor* happy to collaborate?" Cândido said to the scientist as the waiter took their plates.

"*Por favor*, no need to call me *senhor*. If it's a serious project, count me in. I've had it up to here with scientific magazines that do their best to prevent mere mortals from accessing knowledge, as if knowledge of new discoveries were something to be kept in a bell jar and made available only to a select few. Long live the democracy of knowledge!" he proclaimed. "I know things the chefs in this restaurant don't know, but then what do I know about how to cook *bacalhau* in *leite de coco*? There's no doubt about it: my survival depends more on their work than theirs does on mine."

"Alas, I fear I'm not the right person for the job," said Cândido, his spirit bruised by Bramante's enthusiasm.

Lassale tried to encourage him.

"*Ora*, you know all about spiritual traditions! Plus you know how to write. And have no fear: you'll have at your disposal a room equipped with the very latest in multimedia technology. This thing's going to be a great success, I'm sure of it."

THE BROOM

It was late by the time Cândido passed through Lapa on his way back to the hotel. A tram sparkled brightly on the Arcos, as if a jewellery box were crossing the aqueduct. Prostitutes and transvestites competed for business on the pavements, their make-up iridescent under the multicoloured neon lights of the nightclubs. They stared with lascivious eyes into the cars that cruised slowly by between Igreja do Carmo and Passeio Público.

115

Vagrants and children fearlessly trawled through rubbish bags and dustbins, disturbing rats and cockroaches. Passers-by hurried stiffly along, as if trying to get across a war zone unharmed. Long queues formed on the pavement by the park, sleepy heads waiting for buses home.

When he got to the hotel, Cândido bumped into Pacheco in the lobby. He noticed Dona Dinó's broom leaning unattended against the wall by the front door. After dropping his briefcase and helmet off in his room, he headed back to the water cooler in the dining room. The broom had now moved and was resting by the door to the TV lounge. Cândido couldn't believe Pacheco would dare violate one of the landlady's cast-iron rules.

When Cândido went back to his room, the broom was gone from outside the television lounge. He decided someone must be fooling around, trying to have some fun at his expense. Pacheco was slumped in an armchair in front of the TV, nibbling a sandwich and carefully following a debate about the economy. Osíris was asleep on the rug, curled up in a ball.

As Cândido reached for the handle on the door to his room, he thought he saw the broom again out of the corner of his eye: it seemed to pass by the end of the half-lit corridor, walking on the tips of its *piaçaba* fibres. Cândido stopped and rubbed his eyes, assuming it to have been an optical illusion brought on by a cocktail of *vinho, camarões* and hot lemon water.

3   *Ruses*

Delegado Olinto Del Bosco landed at Governador Valadares airport on a clear-skied, humid morning, no nearer to solving the case than he had been when the investigation began. They still hadn't even identified the murder weapon. In fact, the only thing about the case that could be said with any certainty was that his head was now on the line. If he didn't solve the mystery soon, he could forget his dreams of career promotion. The likelihood of him being transferred to a desk job at the Secretaria de Segurança Pública grew stronger by the day.

SIDES OF THE COIN

The information Del Bosco gathered from his enquiries in conjunction with the Vale do Rio Doce police force was not very encouraging. Marçal Joviano de Souza had been a quiet functionary at the local tax office in Governador Valadares, generally admired by colleagues and respected by the wholesalers and retailers whose accounts he handled. He had no children, thus passing on the legacy of human misery to no other creature. He liked to wear a light-brown three-piece linen suit most days, switching it for a white one on Sundays. He had been resigned and dedicated, in roughly equal measure, to his wife and her incurable melancholy.

He spent his not inconsiderable spare time making trips to Teófilo Otoni, where he indulged his passion for collecting semi-precious stones. His wife stayed at home, sitting in the corner of the room, staring into space. Her reflection stared back from the glass of the display cabinets he kept his gemstones in: dishevelled hair, sweaty hands, trembling fingers, a lifeless face with a thread of drool spilling out of the corner of her mouth – a mouth that babbled disconnected words.

Every couple of months, Marçal boarded a bus for Rio de Janeiro. He told friends he was visiting a half-brother on his father's side, whose existence he'd only learned of shortly before retirement. In fact, he touted his gemstones around by day and frequented Copacabana nightclubs by night, blowing all the money he earned as a travelling salesman on strip shows.

After his wife suffered a seizure and died, Marçal bid the little town of Governador Valadares farewell. The half-brother, Marçal alleged, was ill and needed looking after.

In Teófilo Otoni, Del Bosco uncovered further facets to Seu Marçal's personality. The detective was able to confirm that Marçal did indeed buy gemstones destined for resale, but he also discovered that the pedlar never stayed in any of the town's hotels or pensions. Instead, Marçal spent his nights at the most celebrated brothel in the county, the Veio de Ouro, where he was entertained by female friends and confidantes.

These friends and confidantes were left in a state of shock when Del Bosco told them of Marçal's tragic demise. A spendthrift in matters of the pocket and heart, the gentle old giant had always been generous with the girls, treating them like princesses, amusing them with improbable stories. Cornélia, the *cafetina*, burst into floods of tears and ordered that the girls wear black lingerie for seven days as a mark of respect. Marilúcia lit a candle to the image of São Jorge that hung above the mirror in the lounge. Francinete decreed a suspension, for a period of one month, of certain liberties granted to regular customers.

Del Bosco conducted interviews with numerous gemstone prospectors and dealers. None of them had a bad word to say about Seu Marçal. There was nothing to suggest the man had any enemies.

The mystery remained up in the air.

4   *Reveries*

Cândido arrived at the publisher's just as the new multimedia system was being installed. Lassale was trying to be pally with the joiner, who was busy with rulers, tape measures, chords and scissors, taking measurements for fittings. A woman with a dark tan and a gypsy ring in her left ear was leaning against the window, watching them work. She observed them in an aloof but unpretentious fashion, someone who simply preferred to take a back seat in new situations. The room smelled of new.

The woman placed her right knee on the floor and took a piece of equipment out of one of the boxes that lay scattered about the room. Her blouse hung loose at the neck. Cândido could distinctly see the firm shape of her breasts as she bent. Her skirt hitched up over her thigh and her pretty right knee popped into view. Cândido assumed she was a technician from the IT company. He went over to see if he could help.

As he approached, he slipped on some polystyrene packaging. His body tipped backwards then swung forwards, until he lost his balance and landed right on top of the woman. She fell back onto her behind, Cândido's knees splayed either side of her thighs. The hem of her skirt rode up to her waist, exposing pink underwear. Cândido steadied himself, putting all his weight on the knee nearest to the wall, and reached out a hand to help her up.

INTERLUDE

"She's gorgeous!" said Odidnac with a cheeky smile. "Sweet like chocolate."

"Calm down," said Cândido, blushing. "Pretend you didn't see anything."

THE PRICE OF A PERSON

"*Santo Cristo!*" yelled Lassale, running over to help. "You and Mônica can roll around in the hay all you want, but not in here! Do you know how much this thing costs? Seven thousand dollars!"

The publisher picked up the piece of equipment the woman had been handling, as if lifting a baby from its cot, then laid it down carefully on the table.

"My apologies," Cândido said to her. "And nice to meet you. I'm Cândido Oliveira, the writer."

She rearranged the neck of her blouse with one hand and greeted him with the other, smiling all the while.

"Despite the fall, the pleasure's all mine. I'm Mônica Kundali, the anthropologist." Then she looked in Lassale's direction and added, "*Senhor* is the one who should be apologizing for suggesting we're not worth seven thousand dollars between us!"

The publisher smiled awkwardly and said:

"Why don't you both go and get a coffee?"

Cândido took a proper look at Mônica once they were in the kitchen. She was a little shorter than him and had mauve-coloured lips, dark eyes and a face that suggested indigenous roots, an impression accentuated by straight black hair that ran down past her shoulders.

BURNING SPARK

The collision left its mark on Cândido. His soul had been pricked, painlessly and bloodlessly, as if a stiletto had pierced his heart. He was surprised to discover that he now carried another person within him.

Back in his room at the hotel, propped up against his pillows on the bed, his eyes scanned Moderandi's *Tratado Geral da Sexualidade Humana* while his mind distractedly evoked the dark-haired girl. He was troubled by a nagging thought: how could such an everyday incident have got so indelibly under his skin?

He'd not been so smitten since Cibele, a girl he'd known long before entering the monastery. A schoolmate with bright blue eyes, Cibele had been the focus of his youthful passions. For the first time he experienced the wonder of one woman eclipsing all others. Everything that emanated from her seemed extraordinary to him: her shy smile, the way she ran her hand through her hair, the tiny steps of her walk, her habit of holding her school books up to her rising breasts. The road she lived on acquired a special perfume that only he breathed. He would walk down it two or three times a day, reading hidden signals in the laundry that hung outside her house.

Cibele acquired untold dimensions in his eyes. She was the most beautiful, most sweet, most attractive young woman in all the world. And he was the happiest young man.

Nevertheless, the relationship failed to survive the onset of adulthood. Once the initial rapture had died down and the light of their passion dimmed, the dull realities of daily life brought incompatibilities into view. Arguments became more common than displays of affection and their temperaments revealed themselves to be opposite. She wanted to go out when he wanted to stay in; she would insist they went to a club, and he'd be denied the pleasure of their spending time alone together listening to music; he would sit in the parlour, humouring her parents or leafing through magazines, while she spent hours in the bedroom on the phone to her friends. As with so many adolescent crushes, their love didn't stand the test of time.

Then there was Ângela, from ten o'clock Sunday Mass. She had peppermint eyes and a habit of nibbling the little finger on her right hand. She was very pretty: what a joy to praise the Creator for such a wonderful creature! Cândido would look down on her from the back row of the choir, lost in reverie as *O Gordo* bawled out his sermon.

"Concupiscence is the mother of all temptation. We think something looks nice, but that look turns to desire, desire turns to greed and soon we're gripped by lustful thoughts and acts. Look at your neighbour's wife with the eyes, never with the heart. He who burns with desire in this world will burn in hell in the next."

The abbot's booming homilies failed to penetrate his disciple's thoughts. Cândido was too wrapped up in his contemplation of beauty, his almost ecstatic appreciation of the sublime being that lay before him.

While the preacher dealt with darkness, Cândido felt himself drawn to the luminous glow that emanated from Ângela's mane of golden hair.

And anyway, *O Gordo* was always speaking of heaven, but why not listen to the heart here on earth?

Once Mass was over, everything evaporated like a mirage. Cândido went back to the dark and foreboding cloisters. He sought respite and refuge in mythological texts that instructed him on how to conquer his feelings, how to control his mind and the flow of his breathing, relax the body and live a life of asceticism. Feeling like Sisyphus, he'd start to climb Jacob's ladder once more, with a determination as great as his sense of guilt.

But soon, prompted by the memory of a finger being bitten, lustful urges blew the gates of his mind open and the horse of his body bolted. He headed for the toilets, where the voracity with which he feasted on Paradise's apple yet again prevented him from entering the Garden of Eden.

Eventually, convinced that God had chosen not to afford him a monastic vocation, he decided to abandon the frock.

BRIDE'S VEIL

Cândido started to walk past Ângela's house two or three times a day. After seven days, the girl appeared at the door. Cândido stood paralysed on the other side of the road. She was like a vision, an angel from Lucifer's entourage. He was blinded by her splendour. His insides became impregnated with every detail of her face: lips, tongue, nose, eyes and hair. He knew her body's bulges and swells by heart. He divined her perfume, her heat and vibrations.

When he crossed the road, it was as if he were crossing a desert after sighting an oasis.

"So nice to see *senhorita*," he stuttered, his heart leaping.

Ângela smiled.

"Have you left the monastery?"

Her delicate voice betrayed a mixture of curiosity and fear. She was also attracted to him, but she didn't want to be accused of stealing away one of God's ministers.

"I didn't have the calling," Cândido said, trying to put her at ease. "I didn't leave the cloisters because of you. It was because of me. God didn't create me to live alone."

Cândido went back the following day, and the day after that, and every day for the rest of the week. The girl's parents watched on approvingly, judging him to be a suitor of pedigree, and the relationship advanced from the gatepost to the veranda. Cândido's hands also advanced, onto the girl's curves, as their lips met and their mouths fed words to one another.

"I can't stand it any more," said Cândido one night, as his seed oozed out into Ângela's hand.

"But what can we do?" she said. "There's nowhere in town we can go to be alone."

They planned an outing for the Sunday morning. Cândido called for her before sunrise and they set off on bicycles to the waterfall.

They had to abandon their bikes as the road thinned first into a track, then into an overgrown path. Cândido burrowed through the thicket – rucksack on back, Ângela on his trail – and headed for the sound of the water.

The Véu da Noiva soon came into sight, a curtain of water falling like a bride's veil into a bubbling bath before weaving its way over smooth, shiny black pebbles as the river retook its course.

Cândido spread a red towel out over the moist grass. Ângela hugged him from behind, kissing the back of his neck and unbuttoning his shirt. He turned, moving his lips to hers. He slipped his hands inside her blouse and fondled her breasts. Their bodies became voracious, their clothes flew in the air, landing on top of bushes; their minds sizzled with excitement and time stood still, the hands of the clock pointing to infinity.

Their cries of pleasure were drowned out by the thunder of the falling water and the fizz of the spray on the pebbles.

WHIMS

"No argument is without flaw, no flame is everlasting," Cândido muttered to himself when Ângela said she wouldn't give herself to him again until their marriage date was set. "I've told you a thousand times before," he said, "we can't get married now."

"But why not?"

"Because I'm hardly in a position to realize my dreams on my miserly teacher's salary."

"You'll be head of the school soon, *meu amor.* Then you'll be able to buy a *fazenda* and earn lots of money raising cattle," said Ângela.

Cândido said nothing. There was an abyss between his plans and hers. He didn't aspire to wealth or power. He'd be happy as long as he had his daily bread and a few books to read, and could look at himself in the mirror and feel no shame.

Despite their disagreements, they got engaged and exchanged rings, conscious that married life would be a matter of taking the rough with the smooth.

They never got as far as the altar. The relationship lasted until the night they went to the town club and Ângela's eyes began to dance to the tune of a young and prosperous *fazendeiro*.

And now here was Cândido lying in bed, his heart punctured by a spark that had flown off Mônica and lodged inside him.

5   *Trajectories*

Dona Dinó confronted Pacheco over breakfast.

"Stop staring at my broom!"

"I was only looking," he said in a jittery voice.

"*Ora*, I don't like the way *senhor* is looking," the old lady said, drying her hands on her apron. "Has *senhor* got a problem with my broom?"

Pacheco opted for a change of tack. "Any developments in the Marçal case?"

"The detective is back from Minas. He called last night," Dona Dinó said. "No new leads, but he did find out Marçal was rather given to ladies of the night."

"Or they were rather given to him," said Diamante Negro at the end of the table.

Dona Dinó pretended not to hear. She carried on.

"*Ora*, we all know he liked looking at *garotas*. I'm no spring chicken and he used to ogle me. Dirty *velho!*" she snarled.

Cândido stared into his *café com leite* and chomped his bread. It was dry and tasted of maggoty flour. He had an appointment at Doutor Bramante's house, in Botafogo. He didn't want to be late.

THE VISIT

Fluffy clouds made the May sky look like a cotton field and a cool breeze spoke of winter as Cândido made his way through Glória. There was a Saturday-afternoon calm about the place, with its cool shade and lack of city-centre bustle. He walked alongside the balustrade that had once given on to the sea. The city had long since expanded, reclaiming land from the waves, but there were still plenty of signs of old Rio to take in. Cândido glanced up at the Krussmawn clock, its granite column pointing the way to Largo da Glória, and carried on along Rua Catete.

Dodging street hawkers and building work, he passed the Palácio das Águias, a Parisian street corner lost in the tropics. He skirted Largo do Machado and at Botafogo beach fell in with the crowds of students flocking to classes. He could just make out the hunchbacked outline of Pão de Açúcar through the treetops as he struck out along the traffic-clogged Rua São Clemente, towards the welcoming arms of Christ atop the Corcovado.

The front door was almost totally hidden by a riotous bougainvillea with crimson flowers.

"You're early!" said Bramante as he opened the door.

"Like all good Mineiros, I get to the station before the train's been commissioned," said Cândido, realizing he was almost an hour early for their appointment. "Your wife not home?"

"*Não*, Paloma leaves first thing," said the scientist. "She teaches in the mornings."

COEXISTENCE

Bramante and Paloma had met at university: she was a student of psychology, he a student of philosophy; they fell in love, but remained intellectual opposites.

Paloma liked to adhere to Freud's parameters and thought philosophy too speculative and lacking in practical application. She would stand on her tiptoes when she argued such points, to compensate for Bramante's height advantage, and gesticulate animatedly with her short arms. She wore her hair brushed to the left. Her eyes sparkled with passion.

Bramante drew admiration and concern from his lecturers in equal measure. He was blessed with an intelligence that bordered on genius, but he fell into deep depressions and would cut himself off from everybody and everything. He was a voracious reader. He tried to convince Paloma that Reich was vastly superior to Freud. He'd go into a terrible sulk – muscles bulging out of his face, forehead creased, eyes glassed over – whenever she refused to acknowledge that philosophy was the queen of all sciences.

In the early years of their marriage, she would complain that he always had his face buried in a book and ignored the household chores. "You're an ignoramus, Paloma," he'd scream. "You expect me to swap Nietzsche for dirty dishes?"

"Don't I swap Freud for them?"

"*Ora*, I need time to reflect, you only have to repeat; my field requires thought, yours is all written down in books," said Bramante. "And anyway, psychoanalytical theories are all well and good, but all you really need to do clinical work is a pair of attentive ears to listen to the mad rantings of the patients."

As their intellectual distance grew, their physical intimacy diminished.

Bramante became frustrated with the new philosophers and turned his interest to other disciplines. Paloma started to think he lived with his head in the clouds. She suggested he see a therapist, but he refused with the full force of his prejudice.

"If I needed someone to listen to my petty perplexities, I'd go to the confessional," he said. "It's cheaper, you don't have to make an appointment and you have the bonus of being granted a place in heaven!"

Paloma took offence and retreated into her studies. She gave classes in the mornings and attended to her consultancy practice in the afternoons. With time, they became two strangers who lived under the same roof, sleeping in separate rooms, speaking to one another only when they had to and never compromising when it came to their polarized opinions.

Bramante regretted having lost Paloma to psychoanalysis of all things. He had the utmost contempt for a discipline that encouraged therapists to rationalize everything, right down to the way you buttered your toast – ideally, in the manner of someone else, he would say sarcastically.

Paloma concluded that Bramante had lost his grip on common sense. Because of the way he stubbornly clung to his eccentric theories, he'd become a sort of intellectual autistic, incapable of listening to opinions that differed even slightly from his own, never mind ones that diverged a good deal from them. All the same, the couple kept up appearances socially, in order to avoid gossip.

DISORDER

Bramante led Cândido round the side of the house to an annex above the garage.

"This is where I work," said Bramante, welcoming his guest into the study. "That is, when I'm not stuck in some research lab or giving classes at the university."

The place looked as if it had been struck by a tornado. Books lay scattered about the floor; papers and diagrams were piled up, gathering dust; slide rules rested on top of empty beer cans; magazines of artistic nudes spilled out over cushions; pipes and their detritus sat on top of computer disks; ashtrays overflowed. A photo of Picasso rehearsing flamenco steps poked out from amid the chaos, arms arched, hands on hips.

Cândido stopped himself from asking Bramante if he'd ever thought about getting a cleaner. The *doutor* motioned with his chin towards an armchair and Cândido sat down, obliged to share a seat with the complete works of Anaïs Nin. In spite of everything, Cândido was curious. He asked about the scientist's background.

"The accent gives me away," said Bramante, "I'm a southerner, a *gaúcho*, but I studied at São Paulo university, graduating first in philosophy and then in sexual biology. I discovered the difference between intellectual and vocational urges in the nick of time." He spoke in a relaxed manner, totally different to the way he'd been at the restaurant.

"Have you always been a researcher?" asked Cândido.

The sexologist turned his face away and scratched his head.

"I gave classes for a few years. But the military stripped me of my university post. I don't know why even to this day, as I'm quite the opposite of political. But anyway, I left the country and went to Geneva, where I got a grant to study as an intern at the European Centre for Sexual Research. When I got back to Brazil, several universities offered me jobs, but I made the mistake of accepting an invitation to become president of the government's national commission for sexually transmitted diseases. I lasted a couple of months before resigning – in no uncertain terms – after clashing in the tourism department with businessmen who funded child prostitution. I... I..."

The scientist stopped and turned his head away, as if unable to find adequate words. He looked back at Cândido with forbidding eyes, then stretched out a hand and picked up an ivory-coloured pipe from a side table.

"*Bem*, let's get down to work," he said, rearranging himself in his armchair.

"At your service," said Cândido. "So, what's the gist of the first instalment?"

"What's the gist?" Bramante said, perplexed. "I thought you provided the outline."

Cândido gave a weak smile.

"I've been working on the spirituality part. You said on the phone you'd provide the outline for the sexuality part – by today."

The scientist puffed hard on his pipe and blew a thick cloud of smoke out of the corner of his mouth.

"*Não*, I've not prepared anything," he said. "Maybe we can switch things round: let's jump in my car, head over to your hotel and go over your spirituality notes together. As it happens, I'm rather curious to see the scene of the crime everyone's talking about."

Cândido grudgingly accepted.

133

IRREVERENCE

When they got to the hotel, they found Dona Dinó and Delegado Del Bosco standing at the entrance, whispering among themselves. Cândido greeted them both and apologized to Bramante that he'd not be able to invite him in to see his room or where Seu Marçal had been decapitated. Bramante sat down to wait in the television lounge. Osíris lay stretched out on the arm of the sofa, eyes closed into a pair of dashes.

Bramante didn't get quite so comfortable. It felt strange to be somewhere that had only recently been the setting of a mysterious murder. He looked around, as if expecting to find some evidence of the tragedy. Then he stood up to take a closer look at the Debret engraving.

When he came back with his notes, Cândido saw Diamante Negro at the end of the corridor. The *transformista* passed the door to the TV lounge and came to a sudden halt. He spun elegantly on his toes, dipped his shoulder and snaked his head round the door, then straightened himself back up and carried on down the corridor, walking his sailor's walk. He burst into the dining room with the palms of his hands raised to his ears.

"Who's the *bicha* with the curly hair?"

Osíris opened and closed his eyes, above such irreverence.

LIGHT THERAPY

Cândido poked his feet out from under the sheet and off the end of the bed. He rolled over to one side and tried to recover the last remnants of sleep. His eyes were closed but his mind was awake. He thought of Mônica. He opened an eyelid and looked at the window. A square-shaped glow penetrated the dark room.

It was hot and stuffy. He got up and opened the window. Sunday sun was already bewitching the city.

After showering, he called Mônica.

"Going to the beach?"

The invitation caught her off guard. She needed time to think. Her silence made Cândido anxious. Sweat began to fill his pores. He feared he was being intrusive.

Mônica quickly sought to answer all the questions that troubled her. Had she expected such an invitation from him? *Sim.* Did she like his company? *Sim.* Would she say he was an interesting guy? *Sim.*

"Why don't you call for me?" she asked.

Her words flooded Cândido with relief.

When Cândido got to Praça do Lido, he gazed out at Copacabana beach, covered in brightly coloured mushrooms and shadowed sunbathers. Some people played ball, others walked in the wash of the sea.

Mônica came out of her building wrapped in a claret-coloured sarong, her eyes hidden behind sunglasses. She had a bag in one hand, a parasol in the other.

They walked down as far as Arpoador, where Cândido volunteered to put the parasol up. He knelt in the sand, digging a hole, while she lay out her towel and took off her sarong. Cândido noticed her black bikini, without daring to look her in the face. Once the parasol was in place, he changed into his Bermudas and sat down beside her.

"I haven't seen the news lately," Mônica said. "Have they solved the murder at your hotel?"

"They haven't found a single clue. We're fed up to the

back teeth of being questioned and having our lives trawled through."

"Why would anyone have killed him?"

"Seu Marçal was a curious character. I don't know if half the things they're now saying about him are true, but from time to time he did disappear. They say he went up to Minas, but who knows? Maybe he was mixed up in some kind of funny business."

"Do you think one of the other guests is involved?" Mônica asked, as she spread sun lotion on her body.

"*Não sei*," said Cândido. "I keep changing my mind. No windows or doors were forced open, so it makes sense that the killer was let in by one of the residents, or maybe Marçal let them in himself. What puzzles me is that they didn't steal anything. It must have been revenge. But revenge for what?"

Mônica crossed her legs at the ankles, dug her toes into the sand and sprang to her feet.

"Shall we go for a dip?"

Cândido got up, too, but said awkwardly, "I'll come with you, but I'll stay in the shallow bit. I'm not a great swimmer and these waves make me nervous."

She smiled, turned and skipped off ahead of him, her feet burning on the hot sand. Cândido watched her from behind.

"She's gorgeous," he sighed.

Cândido walked up to where the sea licked the beach, sprinkling it with crystal droplets. Mônica went on into the water, pausing before the first wave and then taking a short run, arching her back and plunging headfirst under the surface. She emerged on the other side of where the waves broke, stroking and sliding through the water.

A little later, back underneath the parasol, she dried off and made a turban out of her towel.

"What does your work with the street kids involve?" she asked.

"I go to the Casa do Menor once a week," he said, "and read stories to the children. Occasionally I back them up if they get into trouble with the police. The other day, two lads were arrested for stealing a camera in Copacabana. I waited at the police station till they were released."

INTERLUDE

"Have you seen how stunning she's looking this morning, man?"

"I'm lovesick. All the stars and galaxies in the universe are but a tiny speck compared to the size of her presence in my heart."

"Why don't you tell her that?"

"Out of fear, Odid. Fear that she doesn't feel the same way and that I'll frighten her off. I'd die if I drove her away."

"But you're happy to live an illusion?"

"Yes, until my heart explodes."

"Aren't you depriving yourself of the best thing life has to offer?"

"Maybe, Odid. Mônica's presence unsettles me. No matter how hard I try to listen to her and take in what she's saying, I can't stop thinking about how attracted I am to her. It's like an antenna vibrating inside me."

"Let the dog loose, man. Let your universe explode."

"I'm scared of being a nuisance. I'm too insecure, though one thing's for sure: no one's ever turned me inside out like this before."

6 *Confession*

Delegado Olinto Del Bosco walked into the press room of the Secretaria de Segurança Pública wearing a three-piece English cashmere suit. His shirt collar, though elegantly fitted with a pearl-coloured tie, was riding up around his neck. He was clean-shaven, his cheeks were shiny with cologne and his mouth sketched a quietly satisfied smile.

"The captain, come to lift the cup," Marcelo said to the photographer sitting beside him. "Or else a card player confident in his ability to bluff. He looks like several politicians I could name. They try and dazzle us with their fancy suits, perfume and rhetoric, but it's all a cover-up for their empty words and chronic dishonesty."

The room was packed with reporters and cameramen, all come to see the denouement of the mystery of the "Lapa Decapa", as the press had been calling it. The case wouldn't have garnered so much attention if it hadn't been for the fact that it had taken so long for the police to catch the killer. A jumble of wires ran across the table, forming a strange centrepiece, a bouquet of metallic flowers with square stalks and round heads. As Del Bosco sat down, the red eyes of television cameras and Dictaphones blinked on.

Marcelo took a notebook out of a pocket in his waterproof. He chewed the end of his pen nervously. He was willing to bet Del Bosco would accuse Jorge of being Seu Marçal's killer. Two days ago, the caretaker had been called back in for questioning, and he'd not been seen at the hotel since. The motive was what stirred the journalist's curiosity.

Del Bosco took his place next to the Secretário de Segurança, who said a few routine words stressing police efficiency, media responsibility and the *governador*'s personal interest in the case. He thanked everyone, then handed proceedings over to Del Bosco. The detective cleared his throat, adjusted the knot of his tie and opened the file in front of him.

"All murders have the same end result," he said in a flaky voice. "What varies is the cause and the method. After an exacting investigation, evidence has converged to unanimously suggest that Senhor Marçal Joviano de Souza was murdered by someone who had free access about Hotel Brasil. Not a single clue was found to suggest that somebody alien to the establishment could have gained entrance to the victim's room. No door was forced, no window was broken. The forensics, though they found no clear fingerprints, were able to confirm that Seu Marçal welcomed the killer into his domain and left no sign of struggle or of having been attacked."

Del Bosco was pleasantly surprised with the way the words were tripping articulately off his tongue. He looked over at Marcelo, who was lighting a cigarette, before continuing.

"We questioned all the hotel residents, looked into their routines and customs, checked their alibis. We went to Vale do Rio Doce to gain a better understanding of the victim's background. The information we gathered there allowed us to rule out any connection to forgery, the contraband of precious gemstones or mafia links to the trade. Seu Marçal's psychological profile…" – Marcelo coughed up a lungful of smoke when he heard this: Del Bosco attempting to pass himself off as some kind of erudite! – "…shows that he possessed the typical characteristics of what one might call, to use the jargon of the press, a pervert. His advanced age and lack of resources no doubt made it hard for him to realize his abnormal sexual fantasies."

Del Bosco noticed the way Marcelo was smiling without opening his lips. This threw him off his stride for a moment. He turned to gaze upon the mob of reporters who stood transfixed, holding their breath waiting for the verdict, for the name they could pounce on like a pack of wolves.

"After a thorough investigation, which left no stone unturned and yielded a huge body of evidence, Jorge Maldonado, the hotel caretaker, revised his initial statement and admitted that Seu Marçal had made an unwanted pass at him."

Del Bosco stuck his chest out and gave his arms a stretch as he opened the file before him.

"I will now read the accused's statement: 'One night, after finishing cleaning the kitchen, I felt someone tug at my ponytail. I turned around and saw Seu Marçal. "What is it, *velho?*" I asked angrily. He started with this silly talk, saying my ponytail was sexy, and other things I didn't want to hear. It made my blood boil. I grabbed a kitchen knife from the draining board, held him by the neck and led him to my room. Overcome with hatred, I stuck the knife into him, then cut off his head. I even tore out his eyeballs so that he'd learn, in the depths of whatever godforsaken hell he was in, never to look at a man as if he were a woman.'"

Del Bosco put the papers back down on the table and leaned back in his chair.

"Questions?"

The reporters rushed up to the table. They wanted to know when the criminal would be presented to the press. The detective explained that parallel inquiries and mental-health examinations were ongoing and that Jorge Maldonado would be kept away from the cameras until all police investigations had drawn to a close.

Marcelo remained in his seat, staring hard at the smoke that rose from the tip of his cigarette. Del Bosco looked over at him. It made him uncomfortable to see the journalist so apparently indifferent to the outcome of the case.

The room gradually emptied, until only a few technicians were left, gathering up wires and equipment. Del Bosco made his way down the aisle that cut through the auditorium's seating. He paused when he got to the end of the row where Marcelo was still sitting, absorbed in his notes.

"So, Marcelo, satisfied?" said the detective.

The journalist looked up from his notepad. He spoke with a sigh, making no attempt to disguise the sarcasm in his voice.

"I'm surprised that an intelligent and well-read man such as yourself, Olinto, would resort to the caretaker for want of a butler."

The detective went red and hurried away.

A MATTER OF METHOD

"So, Jorge, who killed Seu Marçal?" asked Del Bosco.

The detective had called the hotel caretaker in again. Media pressure was mounting. The police simply had to close the case.

"I've already told *senhor*. I know *nada*."

Two thickset men entered the room and stood behind the suspect. Jorge felt his stomach turn, his strength drain out of him. His shoulders went rigid, his head filled with throbbing pain and his face waxed over.

The detective furrowed his brow and quickly stood up, letting his seat fall crashing down behind him. He walked restlessly from one side of the room to the other.

"Jorge, I've had it up to here with this. We've got concrete evidence that you killed Seu Marçal. We've ways to make a person talk, you know!"

The caretaker fell to his knees, terrified. He held out his arms, the palms of his hands glued together, and looked up imploringly at Del Bosco.

"*Senhor*, I swear, on *tudo quanto é santo*, I didn't kill Seu Marçal. I'm innocent. I know *nada*!"

Del Bosco looked over at the two men.

"Take him away."

That was at two o'clock in the afternoon.

By eight o'clock that night, Jorge Maldonado had been dragged through the seven seas, thrown over seven waterfalls, made to swallow the contents of seven latrines, subjected to seventy-seven electric shocks and felt the seven thousand substances that nourish the body pour out of his anus and mouth. He was then strapped to a seven-hundred-ton locomotive destined to travel through every pain known to man and pass through tunnels of new and unknown horrors. He decided to pull the emergency chord before he reached the final destination.

He signed all the papers and fell immediately into a deep sleep.

III

CROSSED WIRES

1   *The Escape*

Cândido got an urgent phone call from the Casa do Menor on Sunday night: juvenile delinquents had escaped en masse from the João Luís Alves and Stela Maris reform schools on Ilha do Governador. Cândido jumped on his motorbike and headed straight over.

It was a clear night, the sky thick with stars. The Linha Vermelha expressway was jammed on one side as people returned to the city after a weekend away.

Coloured lights came into view. Estrada dos Canários had been blocked off with police cars, and flashes of blue and red bounced intermittently off the tarmac.

Polícia Militar motorcycles cut through the clogged traffic with their sirens blaring, radio patrol cars mounted pavements and everywhere people rushed around, trying to figure out what was going on.

Cândido went over to where a group of bystanders had formed. They were pressed up against a police barrier, beyond which only authorized personnel went. Those who had gathered informed him that around a hundred boys and girls had escaped from their correction facilities.

LIGHTS OUT

Bola asked the friend he shared the corner with to keep an eye on his shoeshine box. His stomach was rumbling and his head was melting under the fierce morning sun. The whites of his eyes glowed red.

He joined the human ant trail moving through Nilópolis town centre, then ducked into a dark corner. He licked the end of his thumb and counted the money: six bucks. Three more and his mum would be happy. She'd stuff the takings into the left cup of her bra and light a candle to Judas Tadeu. Then, as soon as night fell, she'd blow it all on *cachaça*.

The poor thing, she'd suffered so much! *Graças a Deus*, that monster had finally taken off and left them, thought Bola with relief. His mother had no choice but to turn the odd trick: she couldn't go out to work as there was no one else to look after Chico, Bola's older brother. Chico was now ten, but he hadn't walked since he was six.

The day Chico was to go and get his vaccine, their father beat their mother for putting the radio on. It wasn't because of the music – that he could stand – but rather the constant buzz and jabber – news stories he didn't understand. It was a whirring that seemed to pluck the termites out of the walls of their *barraco* and place them inside his head, where they gnawed at his brain, burrowed holes in his thoughts and nagged at his nerves.

Their father lost control and Chico lost his chance to go and get vaccinated. After that, the illness stunted the growth in his legs. He lay in bed all day, dreaming of owning a proper wheelchair and being able to go out in the street. His mother had made one out of an empty crate and a pram she'd found in the rubbish, but it was ugly and uncomfortable.

Bola stopped in front of a *confeitaria* and stared longingly in through the window. Cashew nuts: too expensive. But what was that next to them? Ugh! Prunes: disgusting! If I spend a couple of bucks now I'll easily earn them back shining shoes later. But if I begged, would they give?...

The shopkeeper watched from behind the cash register, frown on his forehead, eyebrows raised, face muscles stiff. The varicose veins in his legs were starting to hurt. He saw the boy press his chubby little face against the shop window and flatten his nose against the glass. The shopkeeper's hairs stood on end as he imagined the boy headbutting the window or kicking it in, smashing the glass and making off with the chocolate bars.

He signalled to the security guard out on the pavement. The guard had already clocked Bola and had him under surveillance. The guard on the opposite corner got the nod. The boy was suddenly surrounded.

Bola was dragged through the shop, accused of being a thief. He protested, swore, screamed that it was not like that. He tried to explain himself again amid the rubbish bins at the back of the shop, but before he got a chance his lights went out. Pain shot through his muscles, the ground turned upside down, and he was spitting petals of blood.

A MERE CITIZEN

The fugitives had made a hole in the wall that separated João Luís Alves, a borstal for boys, from Stela Maris, a reformatory for girls. They'd joined forces and broken out, fleeing into the Morro do Barbante *favela*, which was now crawling with police.

Cândido watched two soldiers run past chasing a girl, truncheons at the ready. He leaned forward on his motorbike and tried to follow the two shapes with his eyes, but they disappeared into the skeleton of a building under construction.

A woman's voice shouted from a top-floor window:

"Stop hitting those poor *moleques!*"

Outraged by what he was seeing, Cândido drove forward and pulled up alongside the police vehicles.

"Who's in charge here?" he asked.

"Coronel Troncoso," the policeman answered. "Why? Is *senhor* police? If not, hop it."

Cândido walked over to a group of military police huddled around a jeep. Its aerial was taller than the trees.

"I need to speak to Coronel Troncoso."

"Coronel," bawled a policeman, "someone here to see *senhor!*"

The *coronel* put a kepi on his head, jumped down from the jeep and walked over to meet Cândido. An officer behind him shouted orders at a group of soldiers:

"Bring Bia back, whatever it takes!"

The *coronel* came up to the rope cordon, where Cândido stood waiting nervously.

"How can I help?" he said in a dry tone.

"I'd like to request that *senhor,*" said Cândido in an unsteady voice, "tell his soldiers to stop beating up minors."

"And *senhor* is who exactly?" replied the *polícia militar,* annoyed.

"Cândido Oliveira, a mere citizen."

Troncoso furrowed his brow, puffed out his chest and deepened his voice. He leaned in so close Cândido could smell his breath.

"And tell me something, citizen, who's going to recover the physical integrity of the government functionaries who've just been stabbed by the leaders of this mutiny? Is *senhor* going to do it?"

The *coronel* turned and walked away, back to the jeep to coordinate the search via radio.

THE BREAK-IN

The car flashed its headlights as it went by. Soslaio checked the time: 3.35 a.m. The coast was clear.

He jumped like a cat out of the tree and onto the wall. A dog howled at the moon in the next garden and Soslaio froze for a moment. He kept himself flat, face pressed against the whitewash of the wall. He took a little can out of his pocket and had another sniff of glue, then dragged himself along, grazing his arms on the rough cement. He pushed himself up until he was crouching, then made a quick calculation: force of propulsion divided by distance between wall and veranda. He leaped, decisively.

He forced open a gap in the latticed wood with a crowbar, then reached inside and unlocked the door.

He moved furtively, eyes eating up the darkness, guessing at outlines and trying to broaden his field of vision. He banged into a piece of furniture, touched it, felt vinyl and glass at his fingertips. A television. A big, heavy one. There was a chest beside it. He pulled at the drawers and lit a match: papers, a draughts set, cassette tapes.

He pulled a bag out from his waistband, put a few tapes in it. He headed towards the door but collided with a pouffe. He instinctively grit his teeth, as if to repress the sound it made. He tensed his body, clenched his fists.

He climbed the stairs. A stained-glass window refracted the

light of the street lamp outside. He went into the only door that was open – the bathroom. He breathed in the smell of soap. On the side of the sink, next to the toothbrushes, was a wristwatch.

He went back down the stairs and into the lounge, helping himself to silver candlesticks, a clock, a tape recorder and some kind of sculpture made out of acrylic. He regretted not being able to carry the sound system.

He left the house the same way he came in.

Once he was three blocks away, he examined the booty in the light of a closed *farmácia*. The watch was a Rolex. He sucked his stomach in and stuffed the watch in his pants. A car came around the corner.

DIVVIES

Night had recoiled into a dark shade of blue. Day woke shyly on a ruby horizon. Soslaio kept walking. The police car pulled up alongside him and ordered him to stop.

"What you got there?" said one of the policemen.

"*Documentos!*" said the other.

They forced him into the back of the car.

"So then, Soslaio, any good swag today?" the older policeman asked in a friendly tone.

"Not really," said the boy.

"Let's have a look," the younger policeman said, grabbing the bag.

"Clock, tape recorder, a plastic ballerina, candlesticks… You can keep the doll, the cassettes and the tape recorder," the older one said. "We'll have the rest."

"*Tudo bem,*" said Soslaio, resigned.

The younger policeman then held Soslaio by the arms, demobilizing him, while the older man frisked him. Soslaio wriggled and tried to cross his legs.

"What do we have here, then?"

Soslaio looked silently at the Rolex. After dishing out a few slaps punishment, they drove him to the Delegacia da Gávea.

RANSOM

The owner of the house reported the crime the next morning.

"Did they take anything of value?" asked the *delegado*.

"Not much: candlesticks, my daughter's tape recorder... What I really want to get back is my wristwatch," said the victim. "It belonged to my grandfather. It's a diamond-encrusted Rolex Ostra, something of a prized possession."

"We'll see what we can do," said the *delegado*, nodding as he registered the incident.

The next day, the victim got news that the thief, a minor, had been apprehended and was on his way to court. The man was asked to go back to the police station.

"What about the watch?"

"The *rapaz* sold it to a fence," said the *delegado*.

"Can't you track down who bought it?"

"*Senhor*, the police force can barely afford petrol for its cars, much less staff to investigate crimes," he said.

"I'll pay," said the man, seeing what the policeman was getting at. He took a chequebook out from his pocket.

"No cheques, *senhor*," counselled the *delegado*.

The man came back later with cash.

The next day, he got a call from the *delegado*.

"*Senhor*, the fence is demanding big bucks for the Rolex."

"What? Why don't you just arrest him?"

"A thief who buys from a thief should never come to any grief," ventured the policeman. "After all, how does *senhor* think we track down stolen goods and catch *bandidos* who break into other people's homes?"

"Understood," said the interested party.

The watch was returned to its owner and the *delegado* divided the ransom money among his shift team. As punishment for trying to cheat the police, Soslaio was transferred to a borstal on Ilha do Governador. Before being sent on his way, he was given a stern warning.

"Step out of line again and you'll be biting the dirt, catching the breeze via the holes in your body and feeding the worms."

KING OF THE *FAVELA*

Taco got home as the first sunrays grappled with the dark of the night. His grandmother heard him trip over a bucket. She put some water on the stove to make coffee. She sensed his shadow through her cataract and sent him to go and buy bread.

The two of them lived alone together in a tiny *barraco*. She would not tolerate any disobedience from him, but Taco was jumpy that morning. His nostrils were flared, his eyeballs were bulging, his body shook. He'd mugged a *gringo* down by the beach in Copacabana and found a wrap of pure cocaine in the man's leather bumbag.

Taco had big ambitions. He wanted to rule the *favela*, become the Rei da Rocinha, the Al Capone of Rio, the head of the Comando Vermelho, swap his Swiss penknife for an Israeli machine gun.

His grandma stubbornly insisted, "The bread, Taco, go and get the bread."

He didn't want any bread. He didn't want coffee, he didn't want orders, he didn't want Grandma, he didn't want anything. He just wanted to be left alone to enjoy being high and imagining the *favela* kneeling before him, girls fighting over him, gangs bowing to his power.

"Cat got your tongue, *malcriado*?"

He just wanted a little peace and quiet to concentrate on the dreams filling his head. He'd be king of the world.

"Shut your trap, *velha*," he snapped.

His grandmother cursed him. She felt her way uncertainly around the wooden walls, seeking him out to clip him round the ear. He would learn to respect his elders!

Taco reached across the stove to the cast-iron pan that contained the remains of last night's *feijão*. He picked it up and held the wooden handle tight. He stood on the footstool and swung with all his might. The leftover food spattered against the walls. His grandma let out a grunt and collapsed to the floor beside the bed. Her white hair began to tinge with red.

"I am king!" Taco shouted as he threw the pan at the shelves above the cooker, clattering it into tins and jars. An orchestra of metals and glass came tumbling noisily down. He took a slug from a bottle of Alcatrão cognac and lay down on the bed.

He slept for several hours, next to his grandmother who lay unconscious for ever.

DIRECT LINE

At the appointed time, Beatriz removed the layer of mud that covered up the "telephone", the small opening in the wall that separated the two schools. She was greeted by Bola's bright eye peering in from the other side.

"We're all set," breathed the boy.

"Is it really gonna work?" she asked.

"*Garantido*," he assured her.

"Who's gonna take care of the men?"

"Taco's got the box-cutter and me and Soslaio have got knives."

The girl squeezed her mouth closer into the wall and whispered:

"If you need reinforcements, my thirty-eight comes into play."

THE MEETING

Cândido left the area of police operations and drove past a patch of wasteland used as a parking lot by a garage. A high-pitched voice called out to him from behind the crooked metal gate:

"*Tio*, get me outta here!"

He did a quick U-turn and looked in to where the voice had come from. A pair of frightened little eyes poked out of the shadows, like *jabuticaba* berries floating in milk.

"What's the matter?"

"They're gonna get me," said the girl, panicked.

"Were you part of the escape?"

154

"*Sim*. They treat you bad in there, *tio*."

"But… Where am I supposed to take you at this time of night?" said Cândido, talking to himself.

"*Pelo amor de Deus*, don't leave me here, *tio*, the cops'll kill me."

"Do you know the Casa do Menor?"

"*Não*, not there, *tio*, the police'll be watching it."

"Come on," said Cândido, suddenly making up his mind.

The girl slipped through the gate and jumped on the back of the bike. She wrapped her arms tightly around Cândido's waist.

"What's your name?" he asked, as he accelerated away.

"Bia!" she cried. "It's Beatriz, but everyone calls me Bia."

They stopped off at a *padaria* in Humaitá. The warm smell of fresh bread roused their hunger and they ordered *mortadela* sandwiches. At first, Beatriz made Cândido think of a chocolate doll. Her frizzy hair fell unevenly over her thin shoulders and her expression was full of vivacity. But when he looked closer he saw aggression mixed in with the beauty of her face, lines hardened by premature suffering.

There was no way Cândido could take her back to the hotel: it would violate one of Dona Dinó's sacred rules and, besides, the police were still monitoring the place. Instead, he headed for the publisher's.

2   *Estrangements*

When Bramante got home, laden down with Cândido's notes, Paloma was in the garden watering the bougainvillea.

"Did you finish work early?" It wasn't yet eight o'clock and she rarely got home before nine.

Whenever she did finish work early, Paloma met friends for tea, went to the cinema or wandered around the shops. This way she always got home just as Bramante was going out. The *doutor* was a night owl: he was reborn when the sun set; his body bounced with increased energy, his voice gained vibrancy, his mind became more agile.

Paloma turned off the jet that was spraying the mango tree. She looked pale, drained, torpid.

"I've a bit of a fever," she said. "I think I'm coming down with a cold."

Bramante paused at the veranda gate, suddenly feeling sorry for her.

"I'll make you a lemongrass tea," he said.

Ten minutes later, Paloma was sitting at the table with one hand pressed to her forehead, the other holding a steaming cup of tea.

She inhaled the warmth of the infusion. Her face was sad, her eyes floated in tears that wouldn't flow. Bramante looked at his wife, a husband in search of feelings that had extinguished over time.

"What are you working on?" she asked in a miserable voice.

"I accepted a publisher's offer to work on some periodicals."

"About what?"

"Sexuality, spirituality and the crisis of modern living."

To cheer her up, and to assuage his own sense of guilt at feeling so indifferent towards her, he opened the file and spread its contents out on the table before her.

"It's the first chance I've ever had to present my unitarian theories to the general public."

"You still believe in all that?" said Paloma, as she dabbed her thin lips with a paper napkin.

Bramante felt his compassion slipping away.

"My theory now has the backing of a leading anthropologist, Doutora Mônica Kundali. She's working with us on the project. We're going to explain, in layman's terms, the existence and significance of trilobites, crustaceans, reptiles and mammals in human evolution."

Paloma leaned back in her chair and looked at him as if deep in thought, as if able to see through him, through the wall, through the house and out into the backyard.

"And where does spirituality come into all this?" she asked, a little hoarsely.

"*Bem*," Bramante said, straining himself, "Cândido believes that every sexual impulse is an expression of a spiritual force."

"Which you totally disagree with," Paloma cut in.

"That's right, I prefer biochemical explanations. But I think readers will like the idea of sex being a 'liturgy' of the bodies, as Cândido calls it." He underscored the word "liturgy" with sarcasm.

Paloma played with her napkin, folding it up with her little fingers then scrunching it into a ball and dropping it on the saucer.

"And you don't have the courage to stand by your own ideas?" she said.

Bramante put his head in his big hands and ran his fingers through his hair.

"Paloma, I have to earn money somehow. If I was a prisoner of my own thoughts, I'd die of starvation."

She smiled with a mixture of benevolence and disappointment.

"Roberval, you need to start looking after yourself. This ridiculous running around all night like a twenty-year-old has already cost you your classes at the faculty. Your name is mud at the lab – I've had to lie on your behalf! And as for those poor souls who still believe in the great scientist who studied in Europe – the heroic knight errant who renounced a coveted government post on moral grounds – if they only knew you spent your nights researching the anatomies of *putas* and *meninas*!"

Bramante was offended, but he kept silent. He refused to let anger get the better of him like it had last time, a few months ago, when their arguing had culminated in his slapping her in the face. These quarrels were with the therapist, not with her. They were with the psychoanalyst who'd invaded their marriage and estranged him from his wife, his woman, his companion. He didn't want to sleep with a brain, much less discuss and reason with one in bed. He wanted a woman who was hungry for fulfilment in every chamber of her body and soul.

Paloma saw things differently. Her husband had been unable to handle the fading of the sexual tension that had existed between them in their first years of marriage. Their bodies had filled out, their professional lives left little room for amorous leisure and the routine of married life had eaten away at the lust they'd once felt for each other. This didn't trouble her. She'd made an effort to take hold of those threads when they'd loosened and weave them into a web of tenderness and understanding, a web that preserved the love that united them. She saw the life of a couple as a journey through deserts and cities, with moments of darkness and light, silences and raptures. Yet this required both travellers to have a virtue her husband lacked: patient faith in the mystery of love.

He stood up, fleeing the conversation.

"Are you going out?" asked Paloma.

"I've some work to do at Doutora Mônica's house. I shouldn't be back too late."

Paloma picked up her cup and took it over to the sink. She turned the hot tap on and leaned forward, as if to do the dishes. She started sniffling. Bramante couldn't tell if it was because of her cold or because she was crying. He didn't stay to find out.

INEXORABLE

Bramante rolled over into the middle of the bed and stretched out a lazy arm in search of his companion. His hand met with an empty sheet. He was filled with sudden apprehension. He opened his eyes and heard the sound of the shower. He checked his watch on the bedside table. The fluorescent hands showed 3.30 a.m.

He switched the light on. A shower at this time? Was she

feeling unwell? An Ibsen quote came to mind: "Men and women are beings from different ages."

"Mônica, is everything all right?" he asked through the bathroom door.

There was no answer. The shower stopped. He was thirsty, doubtless due to the champagne over dinner. He took a bottle of mineral water out of the *frigobar*, unscrewed the lid with his teeth and drank the bottle down in one.

Mônica came out of the bathroom wrapped in a towel. A loud silence surrounded her.

"Is everything OK?" he asked.

"Sort of," she muttered. "I think it's best if we go now."

Bramante took out another bottle of water and gulped it down. He tried to think of a way to persuade her it was silly to leave at such a godforsaken hour.

"Can't we at least wait until sunrise?" he said, in an almost imploring tone.

But Mônica was already getting dressed. She was in no mood for discussion and she took her time to reply, which made him feel ridiculous standing there naked, his hair dishevelled, his eyes bleary, his belly hanging out.

"I need time to think," she said.

"Have I hurt you?" asked Bramante uncertainly, as if scared of tripping over his own words.

"*Não*, it's nothing to do with you. It's me who's not quite right."

What a whirlwind of emotions, she thought. Maybe I'd have been more relaxed with Cândido... Why do I feel I've been unfaithful to Cândido if there's nothing going on between us? Oh, *meu Deus*, it's all so confusing!

160

MEAT AND POTATOES

Mônica and Bramante had known each other a long time, their paths having crossed at numerous cocktail parties for the academic community, but they'd never become friends. Yet, as soon as Lassale invited them to work together, a game of seduction commenced.

Mônica was on the rebound from a relationship that had, fortunately, not reached the stage of nuptials. She was cautious by nature and especially careful to ignore the advances of scientists, considering it a matter of principle not to form emotional ties with anyone in her professional field. She repeated the old mantra to herself: don't get your meat where you get your potatoes.

Bramante was married and the very idea of coming between a stable relationship repulsed her. Furthermore, she felt particularly disinclined to fall for anyone as intellectually vain as her ex-fiancé, a diplomat who behaved as if he'd been born to wear a top hat and tails. And Bramante was exactly that sort of man: in love with his own ideas and forever showing off the scope of his knowledge – a scope that was as broad as the range of his pipe collection, which only completed the image!

So why did she accept a lift home from him? Was she really that desperate? Her despondency was lessened by the knowledge that there was nothing emotional about it. It was simple physical attraction, that devil of a thing that could break down all resistance and turn expectations on their heads.

SEDUCTION

When she'd asked to look at the pipe he'd placed on the table, Bramante gave her a penetrating stare. There was nothing lecherous about it – he wasn't one of those men who undressed women with their eyes – he merely looked at her in a way that made her feel beautiful. And, like any woman, Mônica enjoyed feeling beautiful in another person's eyes.

As they left the restaurant, Bramante offered to give her a lift home.

Why didn't I raise the barricades then, in the car, when he said I looked *maravilhosa?*

THE MISTAKE

His flattery made her vulnerable. She could see that now, as she pored mercilessly over the facts. If she'd just made an excuse or hailed a taxi she wouldn't be in this situation now, staring at herself in the mirror, being tormented by ghosts of herself multiplied *x*-number of times down a never-ending corridor.

Your next mistake, Mônica, was agreeing to go for a beer!

BEAUTY AND THE BEAST

The day they signed their work contracts with the publisher, Bramante suggested they go for a quick *chope* in Ipanema to celebrate. When she accepted, it was no longer herself speaking. Beauty and the beast did battle inside her head, one dismantling the reasoned framework of the other, a framework that had always led her to avoid chance encounters. Principles, promises, precautions: everything went out the window that afternoon when she climbed into Bramante's car.

"Instead of a *chope*, how about a glass of champagne in Barra?" he suggested.

And you, Mônica, should have insisted on the beer! You fool! You knew full well that, coming from his mouth, Barra meant a motel.

No sooner had they opened the door to their room than they were throwing themselves on the bed, drunk on sensual pleasure, as if the encounter had been predestined. Wild and unhinged, they undressed amid sloppy kisses, their hands running over each other's bodies as they entered a symbiotic embrace that soon exploded into raptures.

TRAP

Why did I agree to sleep with him again? Hadn't I promised myself never to wake up with a man unless I'd been the one who chose him? *Imbecil!*

She knew the second they got to the motel that it would be the last time. Her mind lost itself in riddles trying to justify what was happening.

Why hadn't she called it off there and then? The worst thing was that she'd walked into a trap in the very field in which she was most qualified to avoid traps: the sexual! If she'd given up a diet and tucked into a *feijoada* – if she'd mugged someone at a cash point even, she'd feel less like she'd betrayed herself than she did now.

PERPLEXITY

Bramante stood under the shower, hoping the water and soap would wash away his confusion. How different reality was from theory! Women really were unpredictable beasts!

He was aware that women found him unusually fascinating. To this knowledge, he added his own rule of never approaching a woman who hadn't first shown herself to be interested in him. It rather presumptuously made him feel that he was conceding them some kind of privilege. His area of scientific specialization doubtless stirred female curiosity, creating the impression that he knew secrets and tricks that only the intimacy of the boudoir could reveal.

Nevertheless, he was ashamed of his belly. On an almost daily basis, he made an unsuccessful renewal of his vow to rein in the gluttony and start exercising, recover the athletic build of his youth. And yet he was also aware that women, unlike most men, gravitated more towards brains than physical attributes.

To his mind, sex was a game as engaging as microbiology. Some days you won, some days you lost; it was like bending over a microscope looking for bacteria. He took comfort in what his conquests told him afterwards: because he was married – and happily so, according to the image he portrayed – women who were only interested in a fling didn't find him threatening. While his scientist colleagues spent their free time playing chess or tennis, he was upfront about the fact that he preferred "the smooth and padded arenas of motel rooms".

THE PIPE

When Lassale first pitched the idea to them over dinner in Leblon, Bramante thought the opportunity to work with Mônica Kundali was a gift from heaven. That's not to say he harboured an immediate intention of getting her into bed. He merely appreciated working alongside attractive women, and her beauty had made an impression on him the few times they'd met.

What he hadn't counted on was the winds of seduction blowing so heartily in his favour. Lassale got up to go to the toilet and Mônica asked if she could see his Billiard Square pipe, which he'd just taken out of its leather case.

She picked it up and examined it closely, as if she'd never held such an object before. He stared at her thoughtfully, enjoying her curiosity, and then his sixth sense kicked in. He realized the rest would be a simple matter of skill and patience.

ESCAPE

What made me feel so cheated after the second encounter? Had the meal and the bubbly not been perfectly nice? Could it be that Cândido was casting a shadow? Come on, Mônica, keep a cool head!

She turned the car radio on as they made their way from Barra da Tijuca to Lido, the better to avoid conversation. She leaned back against the headrest, closed her eyes and feigned sleep. Her body travelled faster than the car and she felt herself drifting out of herself, anxious to get home.

Bramante would have liked to ask if they could pencil in another outing, but he kept quiet rather than risk hearing a *não*. The silence made him uncomfortable. It was so thick it would have required a pair of garden shears to cut through it.

"We'll talk at some point," she said as she kissed him goodbye at the door to her building.

3   *The House*

"How old are you?" Cândido asked, while they waited for the nightwatchman to open the gate.

"I turned twelve last week."

The answer sounded meaningless. Beatriz was an undefined age. If she'd said sixteen or seventeen, Cândido would have believed her. Her face and tired eyes were a mixture of woman and child.

"Wow!" she exclaimed when Cândido turned the lights on. She noticed the computer.

"Do they make films here?"

"I'll explain everything tomorrow," said Cândido. "Right now, let's try and figure out a way to get some sleep."

Cândido began fixing the sofa up for her to sleep on and improvizing a bed for himself on the floor out of the leftover polystyrene packaging. As he set about his task, he got Beatriz to tell him about herself.

She didn't know who her parents were, or where she'd been born. She'd been raised in Itaguaí, in an orphanage run by nuns. She'd learned to read thanks to the dedication of Irmã Teresinha, whom she thought of as her real mother.

The nunnery ended up being moved to another city, and the congregation decided to abandon its social work and hand the running of the orphanage over to the State. After suffering abuse at the hands of the new functionaries, Beatriz chose to risk a life on the street.

THE GUN

"*Tio*, if I find Taco, Bola and Soslaio, can I bring 'em here?"

"*Calma*, Bia, I don't even know whether you can stay here, never mind anyone else."

She looked curiously at the bookshelves, at a giant photo of a naked couple on the wall, a globe on a table with curved wooden legs.

"What's that, *tio*? A doll's house?" she asked, pointing at a bulky shape under a plastic cover.

"It's a printer."

"Oh, I nearly stole one once. I held up a video store that had a printer, but it was too heavy. I couldn't carry it."

They lay down in their respective beds.

"*Tio*, can I ask you something?"

"Sure, what is it?"

"Can I give you a kiss?" She jumped on top of him, smacking his face with her wet lips. They hugged each other tight. He felt something hard and pointy scrape against his stomach. Beatriz's eyes were moist with tears.

"What have you got under your clothes there?"

The girl smiled and lifted her top.

"My thirty-eight," she said, showing him the chrome revolver.

"So long as you're staying with me," said Cândido, "I look after this. Agreed?"

Beatriz handed him the gun. Cândido switched off the

lights and rearranged himself, trying to get comfortable, or at least less uncomfortable, on the squeaky polystyrene.

"*Obrigada* for getting me out of this mess, man," Cândido heard the girl whisper.

"No problem, Bia," he replied.

"What?" she said, raising her voice and turning towards him.

"I said you don't have to thank me."

"Huh? I wasn't talking to you."

Cândido propped himself up on his elbow. His eyes tried to make her out in the darkness.

"Who were you talking to, then?"

"God," she said. "I have my dealings with him."

Cândido found it hard to get to sleep. He couldn't stop thinking about what he was going to do about the girl.

WANTED

All the newspapers the next day led with the story of the breakout. Front pages carried colour photos of the guards who'd been stabbed in the escape, one of whom had failed to recover and died shortly after reaching hospital. Rumours abounded that his colleagues had sworn to avenge his death.

According to the authorities, "the ringleader of the rebellion was a minor known as Bia".

Cândido showed Lassale the newspaper, attempting to explain how the girl had come to be at his office. The publisher demanded Cândido get her out of there immediately: he didn't want any trouble with the police.

Cândido showed Beatriz the newspaper, too. She picked it up, terrified, and then slowly read through it, the lines of text dancing in her trembling hands.

"Now what, *tio*?" she asked, directing the question to herself as much as to him. "I swear I never stabbed those guys."

"Now we're going to try and find another place for you, somewhere that will take care of you until the worst of this blows over."

After making a few enquiries, Cândido took her to the Casa do Menor at the Lixão *favela* in Duque de Caxias, just outside Rio. The place was run by Chico Lima, a well-built, middle-aged man with a bright smile and narrow eyes. He welcomed Beatriz enthusiastically, but suggested she take the name Maria while she was there, as a precaution.

"Aren't you gonna stay with me?" the girl asked Cândido.

"*Não*, Bia. But I'll be back to visit."

"Why don't you adopt me? Don't you wanna be my *papai*?"

Cândido felt his heart grow heavy. He chose not to answer.

The girl started to whimper. Cândido felt a mixture of powerlessness and cowardice. Reason and emotion competed inside him, weakening his spirit.

"And my thirty-eight, are you gonna keep it?"

"I promise I'll look after it for you," he said, as he kissed her farewell.

Chico Lima accompanied Cândido to the door.

"Any idea where the boys who led the escape with Bia are?" Cândido asked.

"I know Taco was recaptured. He's in a correctional unit in Bangu. It seems like Soslaio and Bola are still at large." He paused, then added, "I see they finally got the guy who did the beheading at your hotel."

Cândido sighed.

"Yeah, they arrested Jorge, the caretaker. He's confessed to the crime and he's the brother of a *bandido*, but he wouldn't hurt a fly. At least that's the impression I always had."

"Appearances can be deceptive," said Chico Lima.

"You can say that again!" Cândido replied, and went on his way.

INTERLUDE

"Why don't you adopt the girl?" said Odidnac.

Cândido looked at him, perplexed.

"Are you serious? Imagine if I adopted every kid I helped."

"This one's different, man," Odidnac insisted. "She makes you feel all paternal."

CASA DO MENOR

The Lixão *favela* was a human anthill, built in a disorderly fashion atop the city rubbish tip. The residents crowded into *barracos* among tin cans, waste paper, glass bottles, used plastic and excrement. They lived breathing in the nauseating smell of rotting rubbish, competed with vultures and rats for leftover food and gathered scrap metal and pieces of junk to sell to recycling factories.

The Casa do Menor was a big wooden *barracão* in the middle of a yard shaded by *goiaba* trees. The building was structured in an L-shape, the wing nearest the door housing a classroom, games room, TV room and workshop, the wing at the back being home to the bedrooms: girls on one side, boys on the other. The kitchen and bathrooms were stationed where the two wings met and were the only parts of the building made of brick.

Chico Lima ran the place out of idealism. He got nothing

in return beyond the vague hope that his efforts lessened the children's sense of abandonment. The Casa welcomed any needy child, and its "guests" rotated constantly. It was a place where minors could go to sleep, have a shower, get some food, change clothes or keep their belongings.

The bars on the doors were fairly pointless: the Casa was open day and night and the children were free to come and go as they pleased.

4 *Settling Scores*

Soslaio climbed up to the third floor of the Duque de Caxias courthouse. He headed straight for the judge's room. He was known to the functionaries and no one batted an eyelid as he passed.

Juiz Sílvio Truco pulled his overweight body up off the couch and waddled over to greet the skinny little runt with the sad face.

"What news, Soslaio?" said the *juiz*, as he motioned for the boy to sit down.

"Good news," said the boy. He looked older than his eleven years.

"News worth how much?" asked the judge, settling himself deep into the sofa again.

"This time it's gonna cost one hundred dollars."

"One hundred dollars?! You gone *maluco*?" Truco's face filled with blood. "This money doesn't come out of the public purse, you know!"

"I don't care where it comes from," said Soslaio. "I just want my *grana*, like we agreed. I provide the service, you pay."

"We'll see about that," said Sílvio Truco, leaning forward on his belly to get closer and hear better. "What's on the menu?"

"The *menina* who stabbed the guards at the reformatory," he replied.

The judge pushed down on the arms of the sofa and stood up. He wheezed as fat strained at his heart.

"You really know where she is?" he asked, pleased.

"Have I ever played you a bad pass? Do I go in for idle talk?" said Soslaio, irritated that his competence as an informer was being questioned.

"If it proves legit, that kind of information is worth fifty dollars," said the *juiz*.

The boy got up from his chair and made to leave the room, offended by the offer.

"*Calma, calma,*" said Sílvio Truco, his flabby hand grabbing hold of Soslaio's arm. "I'll put your hundred-dollar claim though with the other traders."

Soslaio told him Beatriz was being sheltered at the Casa do Menor and was going by the name of Maria.

FISHING

As soon as the boy left, the *juiz* called the treasurer at the Clube dos Lojistas:

"Melo? We've got fresh fish this week. A bit more expensive than usual."

"Swimming in our waters?" asked the trader.

"*Sim*, an easy catch. A river just near here."

"How much?"

"Two thousand dollars," answered the *juiz*, fully intending to pocket the lot himself.

"Two thousand?!"

"Soslaio produce."

"Oh, ought to be good stuff, then."

"Top quality," the *juiz* assured him.

"In that case, we'll pay," said the shopkeeper.

CARD GAMES

Coronel Troncoso, commander of so-called policing at the Polícia Militar, was a man consumed by ambition. He was short and impetuous. It was a rare *bandido* who remained alive after falling into his hands, and this had seen him rewarded with a meteoric rise through the organization's ranks. But he still found his wage too low for the lifestyle he aspired to.

Pinned to the wall of his office was a *deputado*'s political propaganda poster that proclaimed, "The only thing worth spending on *bandidos* is bullets."

Troncoso had no problem adhering to the code of the Esquadrão da Morte, a death squad that operated on the margins of the law. For every man shot down, he received double his monthly salary.

The phone rang in his office.

"Troncoso speaking," he said emphatically, after being passed the phone by his daily.

"*Coronel*? Melo here. How about a game of cards tonight?"

"A quick hand?" asked the commander.

"Very quick. The table's set, new deck, one life and a straight flush."

THE TRANSFER

At eleven o'clock that night, a metallic-grey car pulled into Praça do Pacificador, in Duque de Caxias. Coronel Troncoso was waiting in his BMW on the other side of the road. He got out and walked over to the grey car. It was occupied by three men, one of whom opened the back door as he approached.

The *coronel*, dressed in plain clothes, climbed in and made himself comfortable, without greeting the others. The car drove away.

The man sitting next to Troncoso passed him a twelve-calibre shotgun, the *coronel*'s favourite. The man then showed him a blown-up photograph of Beatriz.

"*Mulata* scum!" said Troncoso, which prompted a conspiratorial laugh from the other man who, like the *coronel*, was black.

The man sitting in the front passenger seat passed round olive-green balaclavas.

THE KIDNAP

"We want Bia!" yelled the driver of the car, his face now covered. His accomplices ran into the bedrooms.

The kids awoke terrified. They plunged under bunk beds, screaming, or jumped out of windows. Chico Lima shouted "*calma, calma*" and tried to reason with the invaders. A rifle butt to the head sent him flying unconscious to the floor.

Deep in sleep, Beatriz came to in the arms of a man who carried a photo of her in one hand and held her mouth shut with the other.

Linguiça, a boy known for his bravery, ran to her aid, giving chase as her abductor dragged her along the pavement. Coronel Troncoso, covering his partner's back, shot from inside the car. Linguiça's body flew off the ground on impact, his back arching as the bullet ripped a hole through his chest.

They drove off at full pelt, Beatriz held tight between her kidnapper's legs. She tried to wrestle her mouth free, but the hand was strong and held firm. She realized she was going to die and she thought of God.

The car sped towards a junction. A market truck weighed down with vegetables was making its way slowly across the road. The truck had its lights on, but the driver of the car didn't see it until it was too late. There was no time to brake or swerve. The car smashed into the truck's cabin and skidded into its side, flipping it over.

Beatriz flew like a meteorite. When she came round, she was outside the car, covered in cabbage and lettuce. A gash in her arm burned and poured blood. She ignored the wound, picked herself up and ran. She ducked down a side street, and headed towards Avenida Brasil.

She reduced her pace only once she felt she was clear of immediate danger. She was soaked in sweat and panting as if her chest was about to explode. She found a petrol station and ran a rag of alcohol over her arm. She washed her face with water from a window cleaner's bucket and hitched a lift back to Rio in a florist's camper van.

When the doorman opened up the publisher's the next morning, he nearly tripped over the girl asleep on the steps, filthy with blood.

OFFICIAL NOTICE

The newspapers the next day reported that, following a serious road accident, Coronel Troncoso, "the first black man to reach the highest rank of the Polícia Militar" had died. According to the organization's official bulletin, "a gang of minors, fighting over drug sales points, invaded the Casa do Menor in Duque de Caxias and committed a number of atrocities, including the murder of Sérgio da Silva, better known by his nickname, Linguiça.

"As he happened to be in the area, the Coronel felt it his duty to set off in pursuit of the assailants. The car he was in attempted to swerve around a market truck, which was travelling without its lights on across a badly lit crossroads, but the vehicle mishandled.

"Eliardo Troncoso suffered cranial trauma and internal haemorrhaging. He passed away shortly after reaching hospital. The driver of the car, a former Polícia Militar chief, lost the sight in his right eye. Anselmo Silvério, a police informer, had his legs crushed and runs a serious risk of being paralysed. The fourth passenger, a police detective known as Emilinho, suffered minor abrasions."

PRECAUTIONS

Gathered at the cemetery for the funeral, officers and soldiers fired their guns into the air and vowed to avenge the *coronel*'s death.

Cândido explained the situation to Lassale, who reluctantly agreed to let Beatriz stay at the publisher's until a better solution was found.

"But *por favor*, Cândido, get this girl out of here as soon as possible," the publisher begged.

Too terrified to go out into the street, Beatriz made no complaint when Cândido restricted her movements to the office, kitchen and bathroom.

5   *Discovered*

Confined to her hideout, Beatriz played with pieces of paper on the floor, drawing pictures, cutting them up, gluing them together. She liked watching Cândido at the computer, amazed at the images and patterns that filled the screen. She craved meals as if a chronic hunger was sucking at her veins and burning her temples. She missed life on the street, the freedom to sleep on pavements and in *praças*, the pilfering to get by; her gang, their sense of solidarity, sharing glue and weed, cakes and bread. If it hadn't meant risking her life, she'd have gone back to the reformatory rather than being stuck at the publisher's. At least there she could have met up with friends, played games and gone to classes, classes that were always cut short by impatient teachers.

She dreamed of getting her revolver back. Every night, when she was left on her own, she rummaged around the publisher's trying to find it. Everyone was nice to her at Hellas, except for Mônica, who was strangely standoffish.

BOOKS

Bramante came in, carrying a box full of books.

"Tio Barbante," she said, unable as she was to pronounce his name correctly, "what are all those books for?"

179

"To try to understand people," he replied. "To find out about them."

"People like men and women?" said Beatriz. "Why not just ask for their *documentos* like the police do?"

Bramante smiled as he put the box down. He took the books out and started to arrange them into a particular order.

"You must all be very brainy!" the girl went on. "I don't even understand myself, never mind other people."

The *doutor* found this amusing. Doubtless the girl had no idea that she'd just repeated – and with the same sense of irony – the famous doctrine inscribed at the Temple of Delphi by an anonymous Greek sage: "Know thyself." Beatriz picked a book up, chancing upon a copy of the *Kama Sutra*.

"What a funny name, *tio!*" she exclaimed, looking questioningly at the scientist.

"It's Sanskrit, a very ancient language," he told her. "This book, which was written in India around one thousand five hundred years ago, deals with relations between the sexes."

Beatriz chewed gently on her bottom lip, lost in thought.

"Do you need a book to screw?"

"*Ora,* Bia, sex is like lunch or dinner. You can satisfy your hunger with a sandwich at the *boteco* on the corner. But it's altogether tastier if you dine with someone you love, by candlelight, with linen tablecloths, silver cutlery, china plates and crystal wine glasses. Especially if the cook is a master of the culinary arts."

"What's eating dinner got to do with sleeping with someone?" she said.

"Both are better when certain rituals are followed. Sleeping with someone is more pleasurable when the lovers give themselves to each other free from all worry, not even worrying about reaching orgasm."

"Reaching what?" she said, squinting her eyes and frowning.

"Coming, Bia."

"Now you've got me confused, *tio*. The thing about liking a guy, fair enough, I agree with you there. Back in the reformatory, I loved Bola. But we only screwed once, the day of the *olimpíada* between the boys' and girls' schools. In the changing rooms. We screwed to come."

"Maybe, Bia," said Bramante, searching for the right words. "But just as there are many ways to cook chicken for dinner – in a soup, barbecued, *ao molho pardo* or *canja* – there are many different ways to make sexual relations more exciting. In the same way that seasoning improves food, affection increases sexual pleasure."

"Can I say something, *tio*? Promise you won't get mad?"

"Of course, Bia, say whatever you like."

"I think my head is *redonda* like a spinning top. Everything goes round so fast I go crazy. But yours is *quadrada* like a box of books. I like what you're saying, but I don't get it. I was never taught these things. All I know is, when I screw, it's like a weight lifted off my shoulders."

LUNCH

Cândido invited Mônica to have lunch with him and Beatriz in a restaurant near the publisher's. There was no reason to think the Alto da Boa Vista neighbourhood should represent any kind of danger to the girl, and he wanted to straighten things out between her and Mônica. The anthropologist treated Beatriz very harshly. If it hadn't been for the fact that Beatriz was a child and that he considered it wishful thinking, Cândido would have said Mônica was jealous.

Cândido and Mônica shared a roast chicken with *farofa* and *agrião* and both ordered a *caipirinha*. The girl chose spaghetti bolognese. Just being outside filled her with joy; being attended on by waiters and getting to choose a dish was almost too much.

INTERLUDE

"She really is fine, isn't she?"

"Yes, Odid, she's the perfect woman. Not a girl, like Cibele. And she's much more attractive than Ângela was."

"Ângela was good-looking, though."

"She was picture-postcard pretty," said Cândido. "Mônica is like a spiritual love affair."

"Why don't you say that nonsense to her?"

"Are you mad, Odid? Think about how she might react!"

"Come on, man. All women like being told they're attractive," Odidnac insisted.

"They do when it comes from a man they want to hear it from. I'm not sure that's the case with me. And when gallantry comes uncalled for, it too easily leads to friendly sympathy. There's nothing worse than that."

THE CHOICE

Beatriz recounted, in her own way, the conversation she'd had with Bramante, which amused Mônica a good deal. Cândido felt relieved that the tension between the anthropologist and the girl seemed to be lifting.

"*Tia*, what do you think, does the man choose the woman

or the woman choose the man?" Beatriz asked, as the waiter placed a glass of orange juice before her that was nearly as big as her head.

"Women choose men," said Mônica, "even if we sometimes make it look like it's the other way round."

"Why do you say that with such certainty?" said Cândido, intrigued.

Mônica turned to face him.

"The proof lies in a biological phenomenon: the ovum chooses one spermatozoon from the thousand that knock at its door."

Cândido chased a chicken breast around his plate with a knife, unable to pin it down in the oil that seasoned the *agrião*.

"You might be right," he said. "I've never managed to start a relationship with a woman who wasn't interested in me first."

Cândido talked of his past loves, but he could tell Mônica wasn't really listening. She seemed distant, lost in thought, and she never took her eyes off Beatriz. He didn't draw attention to it, as he didn't want to bring up anything sensitive. Mônica accepted another spoonful of rice from the waiter and ordered another orange juice for Beatriz.

Conversation resumed and Beatriz, her mouth smeared with tomato sauce, stared at Mônica, trying to follow what was being said. Then the girl suddenly intervened.

"I hardly understand a word you're saying. But there's one thing I wanna ask you, *tia*, can I?"

"Of course, Bia," Mônica said, turning to face her. "Ask me whatever you like."

"Don't you want to be my *mamãe*?"

Mônica blushed. She leaned right back in her chair and took a deep breath. To buy a little more time, she took a sip of her *caipirinha*. Her black eyes welled with tears. She tried to cover her reaction with a timid smile.

Cândido watched them both in silence, not wanting to get in the way of the intimacy developing between the two females. Mônica stretched both arms out on the table and held the girl's hands.

"I am and always will be your *amiga*, Bia. But what if I agreed to be your mum and then one day your real mum appeared? I try to avoid sticky situations."

INTERLUDE

"Look at her, man. Wouldn't she make a lovely wife? Why don't you and she adopt Bia and start a family?"

"Have you gone mad, Odid?!"

"Admit it, you're proud to be out in public with such a beauty! Have you seen the way guys on other tables have been looking at you, all jealous?"

"They're looking at Bia, Odid. It's not every day a kid like her eats in a restaurant like this."

"Come on, man. Don't be so naive. They're looking at Mônica! Just like you are, devouring her with your eyes: those long fingers, the smooth back of her hands, her gazelle-like neck, her dark face, her wide eyes, her mouth, just made for kissing."

WHAT TO DO?

Cândido faced a dilemma. He couldn't keep Beatriz at the publisher's any longer – Eduardo Lassale had made it clear that the girl's presence had become a problem – but nor could he break one of Dona Dinó's golden rules and take Beatriz to live with him. Moreover, he worried that the girl's presence would draw police attention to the hotel again.

BRUTAL WORLD

The police were still hunting for the young fugitives. Cândido promised to look after Beatriz for as long as she was still at risk. He frantically searched for a new place for her to shelter.

The girl was desperate, vulnerable, frightened of being left alone. She was alive to everything Cândido did, not letting him out of her sight.

"What are you working on, *tio*?" she asked when he sat down at the computer.

"I'm reading Doutor Bramante's study of sexual habits."

"Why don't you just go to a *puteiro*?"

Cândido stopped reading and looked at her.

"For one thing, because it's like playing a game with marked cards. The women fake affection and pleasure when all they're really interested in is the client's money. It's more extortion than it is a relationship."

"Don't I know it!" replied Beatriz.

"Don't you know what?!" Cândido said, alarmed, spinning around in his chair to face her.

"The doorman of a hotel down in Flamengo arranged for some rich *gringos* to screw me," the girl said. "I went up to their apartment, did it with them, took their money and left. I had to share the *grana* with the doorman though."

VIGIL

Everything clouded over, covered with thick fog. Voices and people seemed distant, figures undefined and shadowy. Nothing was vivid except for Mônica, and he contemplated her blissfully. He could make out every twitch of her smile, the vibration of every pore on her face. They were so close he could count the lines on her forehead, the first signs of her first wrinkles. Her teeth, powerfully white, burst forth every time she opened her lips. Her discrete, delicately pointed nose and her eyes, like two black fish floating under arches of eyebrows.

Mônica's image was so clear that it was as if she were an actress filling up the cinema screen and he were a spectator sitting in the front row. Not a single detail escaped him. He could even see the slight deviation in her left eye that obliged her to use glasses for reading.

His focus moved on to her hair, its jasmine perfume. Then he lowered his eyes to enjoy the shape of her breasts, firm beneath crimson silk. At the heart, a slight pinching, as if something was worrying her. He recalled the Song of Songs and mentally recited it:

Thy two breasts are like
two young roes that are twins,
which feed among the lilies.
Until the day break
and the shadows flee away,
I will get me to the mountain of myrrh
and to the hill of frankincense.
Thou art all fair, my Mônica;
there is no spot in thee.

THE VERDICT

Cândido sat at the table, stirring the sugary residue in his cup with a teaspoon. Dona Dinó asked him if he wanted more coffee. He nodded.

"Can I speak to *senhora* for a moment?"

Dona Dinó put the coffee on to warm and dried her hands on her apron. She pulled a chair up next to him, curious and attentive.

"I've got a major problem and I need *senhora*'s help," he said. He spoke with his head bowed, staring at the table. The sun split the table's surface in two. The sunny side was creeping towards an open tub of margarine.

"Don't worry, *meu filho*," she said supportively. "All things in life have their solutions. God takes care of fifty per cent of our problems, time solves the other fifty."

Cândido noticed that the shaded area around the margarine was reducing at an alarming rate.

"There's a street kid called Beatriz who's mixed up in some trouble. She's only twelve years old. The police want her dead. I managed to hide her at the publisher's, but Lassale has had enough. He's worried she'll harm his business. I can't put the girl out on the street. I would like *senhora* to let her live here until I find a proper solution."

The old lady stood up and walked away. She turned off the gas on the bain-marie and picked up the enamel coffee pot, protecting her hand with the end of her apron, and poured Cândido a cup.

"What would we tell the other guests?"

"*Nada*," said Cândido. "If anyone asks, say it's something to do with my work and she's only here temporarily."

Dona Dinó stood in silence by the cooker for what seemed like an eternity. The sun reached the tub and the yellow of the margarine intensified as it melted. Cândido pushed the tub into the shade with the tip of his finger and put the lid on.

"Does *senhor* know," Dona Dinó said in a deep, drawling voice, "that Marçal is still present here in the hotel? Sometimes he passes me in a flash and won't let himself be seen. Bringing a girl here who's wanted by the police would be adding fuel to the fire. But it's also unfair to abandon such a young creature."

Dona Dinó rested one hand on top of the other on the end of her broom. She stiffened her thin arms. Her wilted skin made Cândido think of the cold hams that used to hang in the monastery pantry. The old lady looked down at the joints of her fingers, concentrating so hard she let go of the broom. It fell to her right and banged on the floor with a dry crack.

"I'll make a bed up for the girl in the laundry room out the back," she said, pronouncing her verdict.

EMPTY

Cândido went running up the stairs to the publisher's, anxious to tell Beatriz and Lassale the good news. But the girl wasn't there. He looked for her in the office, the kitchen and the bathroom but couldn't find her anywhere. Then the cleaner told him, "I've just come on the bus and I saw the *garota* hurrying down the road towards Muda."

Cândido rushed into the kitchen, crouched down and ran his hand around the back of the sink fitting. The revolver was gone.

EPIPHANY

Dear Cândido,

Something new is breaking out inside me. I'm glad of your friendship, which is truly a joy to behold. But there's more to this than just a feeling of empathy and trust. Am I in love? Lately, you've been a constant presence in the echoes of my heart. It's not my head that's remembering, mentally replaying a film I've seen. It's more a rousing evocation of your presence. I cannot help but conclude that, besides being a work colleague and friend, you've become a very special person to me.

I assume the feeling is mutual.

Yours,

    Mônica

6   *Spiritual Paths*

Cândido stared at the sheets of paper laid out in front of him. It was stuffy in the hotel room and he felt hot and bothered. He was bare-chested and droplets of sweat clung to the hair on his skin. To his right were the sexologist's notes, to his left the anthropologist's – Mônica's – the woman who dominated his every thought.

He had to transform this jumble of data into something palatable to the public, a task that was hard enough without his concentration being constantly sidetracked by Mônica. It was far easier to correct and rework someone else's text than come up with your own, he concluded. Especially for someone who didn't consider himself blessed with literary talent.

Mônica's smile opened up in his mind. He looked despondently at the computer that Lassale had supplied him with. The screen had gone to sleep; little fish were swimming in an aquarium. He moved the mouse to reactivate it. Mônica popped back into his head. Words and phrases refused to flow from his fingertips. He knew roughly what he wanted to say, what the content should be, but how to say it escaped him. Writer's block before a blank screen.

He made an effort to push Mônica from his thoughts, take hold of an idea and just type. Disconnected words lined up across the screen, confused, illogical. He began the same paragraph three or four times. He compared versions, cut them back, added to them and read them out loud, searching for the right effect, like a musician trying out different chords. Mônica refused to go away. He opened classical texts at random, drank in their style; he listened to music to sharpen his senses. He called upon his muses, tried and tried until he was exhausted, working to the maxim that genius is one per cent inspiration, ninety-nine per cent perspiration.

The publisher was in a hurry and Cândido was under pressure. He felt like a sterile mother whose husband was demanding a child.

HI-TECH DISAGREEMENT

Lassale was hunched over the desk, his head poking out from behind a pile of books and papers, his glasses sliding off the end of his nose. He was visibly displeased. He read as if peering through a magnifying glass and only looked up when he heard Cândido drag a chair over.

"Ah, good, you're here," he sighed.

Cândido nodded a greeting to the publisher.

"Have you had a chance to read the first instalment yet?"

Cândido had handed the final draft in to Lassale's secretary the previous evening.

"I was up until the small hours ploughing through it," Lassale said, as if boasting. "And I have to say, I'm not very satisfied."

Cândido crossed his legs. He tried to hide his disappointment. He wasn't sure how to react.

"This, here," Lassale went on, picking up a bundle of sheets, "reads like a psychology essay. I was hoping for something more consistent and uniform. This is just a mishmash of hypotheses." He threw the reams of paper onto the table, as if rejecting the work of an amateur.

Cândido took a deep breath. He gave himself time to put his thoughts in order and rein in his emotions. When he'd composed himself he said:

"I've tried to make a clear distinction between fact and fiction. With fiction, the author can change the story as much as the publisher wants until it's deemed ready for the marketplace. But for a collection like this we have to be faithful to the facts. Even if our imagination would prefer something different, we have to be true to the data Bramante and Mônica unearthed in their research. They set out a variety of models for human relations, specific to different periods and cultures."

Lassale looked away, weary. None of this bore any relation to what he'd been hoping for. Cândido watched him run his fat fingers through his thick hair, ruffling it on top.

"Maybe the murder and the girl's disappearance are distracting you from your work?" Lassale suggested in a faltering voice.

"The murder has been cleared up. At least officially…" said Cândido.

He knew that neither Beatriz nor the gory goings-on at Hotel Brasil had anything to do with it. What was holding him back was Mônica.

"The collection's thematic range is very broad," said Cândido, avoiding the question. "Perhaps this has prevented the project from having the didactic quality we'd hoped for; the scope just won't allow for it."

"*Sim*," Lassale interrupted him, "but I was hoping for something simpler. As Bramante suggested, something that would jump out from the magazine stand and catch the eye of the executive with the imported car just as much as the domestic maid with her shopping basket." He paused before adding, in a shaky voice, "In this age of uncertainty, what is sex between a man and a woman? How does spirituality come into it?"

This brought Mônica back into Cândido's thoughts.

Lassale leaned over the desk, animated by his own questions.

"What's the common denominator between sexuality and spirituality?"

"The way in which a person is a person derives from his or her concept of God," Cândido suggested. "People differ according to how they differ on this concept."

The publisher cut in, "What about agnostics like me?"

"In the case of agnostics," Cândido said, "it's values and principles that count."

"And how does that apply to sexuality?" asked Lassale, his professional interest now taking a back seat.

"The less guilt a person feels," said Cândido, "the healthier their sex life."

"You're not suggesting," objected Lassale, "that libertines and the depraved serve as our yardsticks?"

"*Não*, of course not," said Cândido. "Their lack of scruples is a matter for psychotherapists like Bramante's wife. What troubles me is the distance that exists between body and spirit, between love for one's partner and love for God."

"And you think," questioned the publisher, "that this distance should disappear?"

Cândido remembered Mônica again.

"*Sim*, I think so," he said, before adding, as if something in the air had set off a chain of memories, "and then we'll be brought into the bed chamber, as the poet inferred, where a hug becomes an embrace, a caress becomes a holy kiss, copulation becomes communion, eroticism becomes agape love, pleasure becomes liturgy."

Lassale leaned back.

"Cândido, such a poetic view of things is so naive!" he said, a sarcastic smile hanging from the corner of his mouth.

Cândido was lost for words. Lassale had just admitted that he didn't believe in his own editorial project.

"The Song of Songs," said Cândido, defending himself, "speaks of this unity and is an erotic text found in the Bible. It's considered the word of God by the faithful."

Lassale fixed his eyes on Cândido; he needed time to process what he'd just heard. But he wasn't ready to let up yet. He returned to more pragmatic terrain.

"What did you do to the parables I gave you?"

"As you'll have seen, I edited and improved them."

"You edited them?! I'm the senior editor here. Anyway, you didn't just rephrase them – you changed them!"

"Isn't that what I'm supposed to be doing?" Cândido protested. "Didn't you say that for the spiritual parts I should employ my own knowledge?"

"*Sim*. But what you've done is change their meaning! Have you any idea how much I paid for them?"

"Paid?" Cândido said, surprised. "What do you mean, paid?"

"Two or three self-help manuscripts land on my desk every week. As a rule, they're badly written regurgitations of old ideas, mere transliterations of ancient Oriental parables. But in among the froth, I find the odd hidden gem. I'm not

194

prepared to publish the whole book, but I buy the story from the author. That's what I passed on to you."

"*Sim*, and I read them all carefully," Cândido replied. "Then made them appropriate to the content of the instalment."

"They were great parables," Lassale exclaimed. "How dare you adulterate them!"

Lassale was starting to stutter. Cândido decided to let the man blow off some steam instead of arguing back.

"You changed the stories!" the publisher complained once more. "Take the parable of the miser."

Lassale dug it out from among the papers on his desk. He held the sheet of paper in his hand and sat back, resting his elbows on the arms of his chair.

"It's a great story, full of wisdom! And you had the nerve to alter it!"

The parable told the story of a man who stored gold bars in his house. A great famine befell the region and when his supply of food ran out he died, desperately trying to eat the gold.

"*Ora*, Lassale," objected Cândido, "how can a story like that mean anything to our readers? For a start, the misers of today don't keep their money at home. That's what banks, safes and tax havens are for."

RECIPE FOR SUCCESS

"I think it's important that the first instalment includes this New Age thing," said the publisher.

Cândido leaned back and scratched his head.

"I'm not very good on the latest fads, Lassale. The way I see it, a new age is a new phase in our lives. I, for example, seem to be entering one now."

Lassale offered him a complicit smile.

"Falling in love?"

"*Não sei*. For now, it's probably just wishful thinking on my part," Cândido said. Not prepared to open up any further, he returned to the main argument. "I don't know about New Age. The Good News, on the other hand, has existed for at least two thousand years – it's there for all to see."

"Perhaps New Age is too broad a spectrum," admitted the publisher. "Why not just focus on the area of medicine, given that so many people are paranoid about their health these days."

"Paranoid about their bodies, you mean," corrected Cândido. "Getting old is seen as having something seriously wrong with you, as if it were an illness."

"My thinking," Lassale went on, "is that we ought at least to mention alternative medicines, something that touches on herbs and physical exercise, diets and transcendental meditation, controlled breathing and spiritual well-being."

Cândido moved about nervously in his chair.

"Lassale, remember the domestic maid you were just talking about?"

The publisher furrowed his brow, squinted his eyes.

"*Bem*," Cândido continued, "how's she supposed to improve her spiritual well-being on her pittance of a salary? Expect her to watch her diet and breathing when she eats in a matter of seconds, anxious to get on with doing the dishes from lunch? Is she to exercise after she's worked all day and spent hours stuck in traffic to get home? Will she have the time and resources to learn transcendental meditation? Can someone who lives in a room too small for physical or psychological intimacy expect a healthy sex life? *Ora*, I prefer the Sermon on the Mount: it's not so elitist."

7   *Crossfires*

He took the bag from the man sitting at the bar and left, vigilant of everything around him. The man tipped his head back and sank the rest of his *chope.* Beatriz ducked behind a lamp post, fearing she might be seen.

She knew the ruse: the bag contained a takeaway lunch, but the gear was hidden under the *feijão,* rice and eggs. She took a bottle of nail polish out of her pocket, unscrewed the cap, held it up to her nose and inhaled deeply. She grew inside herself, her head expanded and a brief dizziness made way for courage. She'd sniffed shoe glue for kicks all her life. Nail polish was for work.

She followed the boy, her sweaty hands tucked into the pockets of her green jacket, her whole being ready to explode with tears of fury. She'd see this battle through to its conclusion. She had a score to settle, a monkey to get off her back. *Graças a Deus,* I'm still alive, she thought. But I should be dead.

He looked back behind him, first over his right shoulder, then over his left. He was jumpy, but he didn't notice he was being followed.

He's probably drunk, she thought. He usually was by that time of day.

The boy slowed his pace as he came on to Rua São João Batista. He held the packed lunch close to his body when he saw a police car pass. He paused at the kerb, checked for traffic in both directions, then crossed. Half a dozen people were queuing outside Santa Rosa cinema. He joined the back of the line.

She hurried, so as not to lose sight of him, causing a bus to sound its horn as she ran across the road. Her heart was racing. She stopped at a news stand opposite the cinema and feigned interest in a magazine on *sertanejo* music. The boy reached the front of the queue and went through the turnstile. She ran over, waited for a couple to pay, then bought a ticket for herself and went in. He'd vanished.

She stood still at the curtain by the door, letting her eyes become accustomed to the light given off by Kevin Costner and the Sioux Indians up on the screen. She'd recognize the boy half blindfolded. She just had to be patient. She knew he was there to pass the gear on to someone else and she knew the drill: the addict never stayed until the end of the film; he paid, picked up, pushed off, desperate to sample the merchandise. She had to keep an eye out for anyone who got up during the film, then look at who was sitting next to the empty chair.

The cinema exploded to the sound of a herd of buffalo running across the screen. Distracted, she almost missed the silhouette as it passed in front of her. He must have been in the toilet. The boy now hovered around the back aisle, craning his neck in search of a particular place or person.

It was now or never. She pulled the gun out of her waistband, held it firm with two hands and screamed:

"Soslaio!"

Rifle fire and stampeding buffalo smothered the cry of her voice, but the boy heard and turned. She fired her first shot. He threw himself to the floor between the guard rail and the last row of seats. She fired again and hit him in the head. The audience didn't know what was going on. It took them a few moments to realize that real shots had mixed in with the ones from the screen, by which time Beatriz had reached the emergency exit and was able to mingle in with the panicked rush to get out of the auditorium.

From the steps of the Primeira Igreja de Batista de São João de Meriti, Beatriz watched as police cars and ambulances surrounded the cinema. She took the bottle of nail polish out of her pocket and painted her nails.

DEPARTURE

Bramante went into the house and closed the door behind him. He took off his shoes and made for the stairs, guessing at shapes in the shadows. He climbed, careful steps combined with false ones, and headed for the bedroom. His head was saturated with alcohol, as if his brain was floating in an aquarium. He was surprised to see a thread of light under Paloma's door. He looked at the hall clock: 2.30 a.m. He made for his bedroom, undressed, went to the bathroom and hauled himself under the shower. He didn't want Paloma seeing him like this. She usually went to bed early. Never before had there been any sign of her being awake when he'd got home in the middle of the night.

He brushed his teeth, wrapped himself in a damp towel and gently knocked on his wife's bedroom door.

"Paloma, you OK?"

The door opened. She was dressed in blue dungarees and a pink shirt and was wearing make-up. He noticed a couple of suitcases open on the bed.

"What's all this?" he asked. "What's going on?"

Paloma went back to packing the suitcases. She answered without looking at him. "I'm leaving, Roberval. I'm catching a seven-o'clock plane."

"Leaving? What do you mean?"

His voice came out husky and bedraggled. Inebriated and naked, he felt fragile in front of this determined woman.

"I've met someone else," Paloma said.

"What?" Bramante exclaimed. "Are you telling me, at this outrageous hour of the morning, that our marriage is over?"

Paloma placed blouses and dresses neatly in the case.

"Do you really need me to tell you that our marriage has been over for a long time?" she said. "If you'd come home last night, you'd have found me ready to talk. So let's avoid scenes and hypocrisy. If your macho pride is wounded, it'll soon heal. My life's with Mário now. We're off to Paris first thing in the morning, on our honeymoon."

Bramante slumped down in a chair. The drink inside him was having a stupefying effect. He would have liked it all to be a bad dream. He stretched out a hand and grabbed a bottle of mineral water from the dresser.

"You're never coming back?" he asked, his voice barely audible.

He felt depressed for the first time since he and Paloma had drifted apart. A sense of bitterness filled his chest. His eyes glistened with tears.

"I'll be back in two weeks," Paloma said. "*Sim*, I'll come back here; there are lots of things we need to sort out together, the house, the car... But *não*, I won't be coming back here to live."

"Paloma, don't you think —"

She interrupted him.

"Sorry, Roberval, but now is not the time. I'm in a hurry and you're in no fit state."

Bramante dabbed his eyes with the tip of the towel, inadvertently revealing his flabby body. His hair hung loose down to his neck, making him look younger than he really was.

"Who's Mário?"

"A colleague, a Lacanian psychoanalyst. We've been lovers for several months."

"Why didn't you tell me sooner?"

"The same reason you never mention the women you get your leg over with before coming home at dawn."

Bramante started to feel cold. His hands shook and sweated at the same time.

"Do you love him?"

"Very much," said Paloma, turning to face her husband for the first time.

"I'll miss you," he said.

Paloma didn't react. She went on arranging clothes in the two suitcases. She was torn between remembering the good times she'd had with Bramante and thinking about what she now felt for Mário. Professional interests had brought her and Mário together in what had seemed like friendship, albeit a very agreeable friendship that had been sucked on like a never-ending sweet. But at a party a few months previously that friendship had expressed itself as an attraction, an attraction that began by showing them that their bodies, though middle-aged, were very much alive, and that their emotions were just waiting to be revitalized. After that, love blossomed like a well-tended plant. There was no mad passion, ecstasy, demands or promises. Just tender gestures, small daily displays of attention, phone calls… the harmonious notes of a symphony in which every instrument played its precise part.

When Paloma called Mário to say she was ready, Bramante was fast asleep, snoring, curled up in his wet towel. She kissed him on the forehead before leaving, like a mother saying farewell to an errant child.

NEEDLE IN A HAYSTACK

When Cândido ordered yet another *caipirinha*, Mônica couldn't contain herself.

"Don't you think you've had enough? Let's pay the bill and get going."

Every day for a month, they'd gone looking for Beatriz together after work. They'd searched Central do Brasil railway station, Praça XV, around the Igreja da Candelária, Passeio Público, Largo do Machado and from Praça General Osório to the end of Leblon. Now they were covering Copacabana, from Forte to Leme.

"You know, Mônica, I feel like such an idiot," Cândido said, once they were back outside on the pavement. "Lassale is demanding another draft of the texts, but all I can think of is finding Bia. I might go out to Itaguaí."

Mônica stopped and stared at him.

"What for?"

"Bia was raised there," he told her, "in a nun's orphanage."

Mônica set off walking again, her eyes glued to the ground.

"If you ask me, you'd be wasting your time," she said. "Bia wouldn't be so stupid as to go to the one place the police know to look."

INTERLUDE

"Why not open up, man? Admit it: Bia is just a pretext for you to spend time with this woman!"

"OK, Odid. I'll have another drink in a minute and then get everything out in the open. I'll tell it to her straight: for some time now, I've been a man with a one-track mind, a man in love with a beautiful woman, a beautiful woman who tells me I've had enough to drink in that wonderful crisp voice of hers, a beautiful woman who fills my heart so much it's no longer me living, but her living inside me."

"That's deep, man."

RAGS

"Mônica, there's something I need to get off my chest. But before I tell you, let me have a nightcap in that bar over there."

She looked at him tenderly. The girl's disappearance had unsettled him. He was afraid Beatriz would fall into the hands of the heavies out to avenge the reformatory breakout and Coronel Troncoso's death.

"*Tudo bem*, Cândido, but let's have the nightcap at my place. It's right around the corner and it's easier to talk there."

They walked on to Lido, scanning the faces of the gangs of kids scattered about the Copacabana pavements: scruffy boys and girls with dirty feet stuffed in flip-flops, busy in violent play, children whose covetous eyes honed in on tourists' handbags and cameras, whose aggressive smiles begged for money from cars at traffic lights and people drinking under awnings outside terrace cafés. The kids all had the same profile – runny noses, burning eyes, soiled skin, sticking-out bones and malnourished bodies that hid their ages – as if they were all exactly the same.

SHOWER

By the time they got to Mônica's apartment, Cândido's shirt was drenched in sweat. The stench of his skin embarrassed him. Mônica showed him into the living room, then disappeared to the kitchen to get some water.

Cândido remained standing for fear of getting the furniture dirty. He looked around the room, taking in the details: a herd of trinket elephants, all with their backs turned to the door, a lush fern spilling out from the window sill, several paintings on the walls.

Mônica came in with two glasses and a bottle of cold water on a tray.

"Sit down, make yourself comfortable," she said.

She bent over to put the tray on the coffee table and Cândido got a glimpse of her breasts. Two ripe fruits. She passed him a glass of water and he gulped it down.

"Mind if I use the bathroom?" he asked, shyness betraying his nerves.

"Out into the corridor, first door on the left," Mônica said, pointing. "Why don't you have a quick shower while I make us a drink?"

For a moment he didn't know how to react. What he'd heard sounded like an invitation to feel less like a guest and more like an intimate friend.

"Or would you prefer a hot coffee after a shower?"

"A coffee would do me some good," he said, watching her open a cupboard in the hall and reach for a towel. She reminded him of Osíris as she stretched. Arms above her head, hands splayed, fingers clawing, she stood on the tips of her toes, her chest pressed flat against the shelves and her back arching in a sensual curve. This feline Mônica stoked his fantasies.

He had never seen a bathroom like it: the walls were lined with Portuguese tiles, watercolours of vintage brands of French perfume hung by the door and glass bottles of cosmetics and talc filled the shelves; there were plants everywhere and the whole place smelled of fresh lavender. Cândido felt overwhelmingly comforted, as if the cleanliness had taken him in its arms and washed away his insecurities.

He undressed with tremendous care, not wanting a single drop of sweat to fall on the ceramic floor. There was nowhere to hang his clothes. He thought about putting some of the bottles on the floor and clearing a space by the sink, but decided instead to fold up his trousers so small they'd fit on the toilet seat and to hang his pants and shirt on the door handle.

He heard Mônica call to him.

"I'll leave you a clean T-shirt outside the door," she said.

"Ah, OK, *obrigado*."

He got into the shower cubicle and was momentarily fazed by all the taps. He tried one. A squirt of water sprayed against his legs. He turned another. A cold gush came down onto his head. He twisted the next knob along and managed to moderate the flow until he was finally able to give his body over to the shower. He soaped his hair and face, threw his head back and opened his mouth underneath the jet as the water rinsed away the foam. He scrubbed soap into his neck and shoulders, under his armpits and down his arms, across his chest and navel, and around his sides as far as his hands could reach. When he was soaping his penis and buttocks, he got excited imagining that Mônica might suddenly come in, naked, asking if he wouldn't mind if they bathed together.

As he dried himself down with a shaggy blue towel, he heard the phone ring. It rang and rang, as if nobody was home. At last he heard a door opening.

"*Sim… sim…* He's here. Now?… What did she say?… Wait a minute, I'll get him." There was a pause and then Mônica shouted: "Cândido, it's the publisher's. Bia's turned up!"

Mônica passed the phone and T-shirt through the half-open door. She saw he was wrapped in a white towel and had made a turban for his hair out of a smaller towel of the same colour.

The security guard from the publisher's told Cândido that the girl had arrived a short while ago and seemed to be under the influence of drugs. She was talking excitedly, confusing what she said and gesticulating a lot. Cândido told the guard not to let her out of his sight.

Cândido said goodbye to Mônica with a kiss on the cheek. She wished him luck. He jumped in a taxi bound for Alto da Boa Vista, clutching a plastic bag containing his dirty shirt.

IN KIND

Beatriz was dressed in brown jeans and a green fake-leather jacket. She was barefoot and her eyes were bloodshot. Her nails were painted bright red. As soon as she caught sight of Cândido, she started to giggle.

"Bia," he said, hugging her. "What happened? Where've you been all this time?"

"*Ora,* I went on a trip, *tio.* A good one! But *tudo bem,* it's all sorted now," she said, between fits of laughter.

Cândido tried to bring her back to reality.

"Why did you disappear? Where are your trainers?"

"I traded them in for this," she said, pulling a tin of glue from her pocket. "It's wild!"

Cândido noticed something bulky in her other pocket.

"And what have you got in there? More glue?"

Beatriz pulled out the revolver, as if surprised to find it.

"You take it, *tio*, chuck it away. I won't be needing it no more. I've replied in kind," she said. She burst out laughing again, totally beside herself.

Cândido sat down and pulled her towards him.

"What happened, Bia? You can tell me. I promise whatever you say will stay between the two of us."

A look of spite darkened the girl's face.

"I wasted Soslaio, the little snitch. By now that *branquelo* will be rotting in hell."

Cândido nearly choked. His body started shaking. He hugged Beatriz tightly as the tears came. They cried in each other's arms.

Back at the hotel, Cândido made up a bed in the room Dona Dinó had set aside for the girl.

"Promise me something, *tio*?" Beatriz asked.

"That depends, Bia. If it's in my power."

"Find Taco and Bola for me."

FLOWERING

Dear Cândido,

I cursed fate when your visit to my flat was cut short by Beatriz's reappearance. I know how much of a relief the news was to you, and it was to me too. But I couldn't help regretting having missed out on the chance of you opening up to me.

In any case, here's what I'd planned to say: I've been thinking about you a lot, about us, and I know that these feelings flowering inside me are stronger than reason and good sense.

The fact of the matter is, I like you very, very much.

Yours,

Mônica

8   *Back to Square One*

Beatriz woke up early and went to find Cândido. She noticed a stain on the floor in the shadows of the corridor. She turned the light on and saw a thick ruby-red liquid: blood. It was flowing out from under one of the bedroom doors.

"*Tio*, wake up, quick!" she urged, banging on Cândido's door.

Cândido opened the door in his pyjamas.

"What is it, Bia?"

"There's blood over there."

Cândido came out into the corridor. He saw Madame Larência, dressed as if for a gala ball, standing dumbstruck before a puddle of blood. She took a deep breath, filled her lungs and screamed:

"*Santa Mãe de Deus!* Dona Dinóóóóó, come here, quickly!"

Soon, all the guests had their heads and torsos poking out into the corridor. Dona Dinó banged hard on the door that was the focus of everyone's attention.

"Doutor Pacheco! Doutor Pacheeeeco!"

She found her copy of the key and fumbled nervously, trying to get it into the lock. The door opened and she froze before what she saw: Pacheco in a rocking chair, dead, his head in his lap, two black holes beneath bushy eyebrows and tortoiseshell glasses.

In a jittery voice, Marcelo said, "He always did run around like a headless chicken."

Diamante Negro gave him a sharp elbow to the ribs.

OBLIVION

"Ah, here's Del Bosco," said Marcelo, "come to beat the killer's name out of Pacheco's dead body."

The detective walked in sheepishly, with Jorge in tow. The caretaker was being returned to freedom, though he looked ragged and traumatized. Del Bosco ignored Marcelo and greeted the forensics team, who were busy setting up their equipment. Then he went over to Dona Dinó.

"I want to talk to the girl."

Cândido stepped in.

"Not until the Juiz de Menores gets here, *delegado*."

Diamante Negro bounded down the corridor.

"*Minha Nossa Senhora dos Aflitos! Santa Mãe de Deus!*"

He threw himself into the detective's arms.

"*Delegado*, why does one never see a *bacalhau* with a head, black twins, a bald beggar, a saint wearing glasses, a dwarf's funeral, an *ex-corrupto*, a mother-in-law's bust on the mantelpiece, a *puta*'s son named Júnior, or police who solve crimes by investigation?"

Del Bosco brusquely shook himself free of the *transformista*.

MANIAS

After learning nothing from Beatriz's testimony before the Juiz de Menores, Del Bosco summoned Madame Larência to the police station.

"*Ora*, does *senhor* seriously think I could chop a man's head off without getting a single drop of blood on my party dress? I just happened to be passing the room when the blood seeped under the door."

"And where had *senhora* been?"

"At a fashion show thrown by the Performance modelling agency," she said, before adding in a confidential tone, "There are always a few girls left over for my market, *senhor*. Clients are very demanding these days. They want girls with soft skin, perfect teeth and light-coloured eyes, but above all they want girls who look healthy. A common cold and the client thinks the girl's got Aids."

Del Bosco found her chatter annoying and considered her forced attempt at familiarity a sign she had something to hide. He decided to put the pressure on.

"Madame Larência, I have it on good authority that *senhora* knows who committed the Hotel Brasil murders."

Her rosy make-up couldn't hide the sudden paleness in her face.

"I haven't the faintest idea who the murderer is, my dear. I do, however, think it's probably some *maluco*, killing just for the fun of it. *Senhor* can't imagine what humans are capable of! I've had clients spread corn out on the floor in order to watch girls peck the ground like hens. Another covered his body in sticking plasters because he got a thrill out of being 'peeled' and having his hairs pulled. I know a businessman

211

who puts a dog collar around his neck and gets the girl to hold the lead while he goes about on all fours and barks and pants with his tongue hanging out."

ACCOMPLICES

"We're back to square one," said Delegado Del Bosco, as he welcomed Cândido in to testify.

"And why did *senhor* think it was Jorge?" asked Cândido.

"After cross-referencing Madame Larência's and Rosaura's statements, I identified Jorge Maldonado as the prime suspect," the detective said. "Then I analysed his psychological profile."

"Has *senhor* studied psychology?" said Cândido, making an effort to contain his sarcasm.

"Experience affords me a certain authority in the field," said Del Bosco. "I deduced that the caretaker was envious of the guests, or motivated by some other despicable reason, but I lacked hard proof. So I asked forensics to examine his fish knife."

"And?"

"They ascertained that the fish knife had different properties to the blade used for the beheadings, which was longer and narrower, like a fencing sword with a longitudinal edge."

"Meaning," said Cândido, "that the forensics were unable to prove *senhor*'s psychological hunch?"

"That's right," Del Bosco admitted, somewhat uncomfortably. "It turns out I was mistaken."

"So why did *senhor* keep Jorge locked up?"

"Because out of fear, before the forensic report came in, Jorge confessed to killing Seu Marçal."

"And what about Pacheco? Do we know for sure it's the same killer?" asked Cândido.

"*Sim*, the laceration was identical on both heads. And once again, nothing was stolen other than the eyeballs. It's the work of a lunatic."

Cândido closed his own eyes in an atavistic act of defence.

"And are there any new clues or suspects?"

The detective got up from his chair and started walking from one side of the room to the other.

"To be frank," said Del Bosco, "I'm as in the dark as the decapitated heads. I'm taking the whole investigation back to the beginning and starting again. We're calling for new statements from all the residents and anyone else who's been in the hotel."

Del Bosco stopped and leaned over the table, his fingers spread wide, his head close to Cândido's. The detective was fighting a feeling of failure.

"Would *senhor* not agree with me that the killer has to be someone from inside the hotel?"

Cândido flinched. He was wary of the detective's tricks.

"*Não sei.* I don't think so. The police have gone down that road once before and been wrong. I sincerely hope the same mistakes aren't made twice. That said, I trust *senhor* will soon have the case wrapped up."

"Don't worry, we're now taking a more scientific approach," said the detective, emphasizing the word "scientific". "Nevertheless, I'll be needing everyone's cooperation. I'd like *senhor* to give me the low-down on Doutor Pacheco."

"I'm sorry to have to disappoint," said Cândido, "but all I know is that Pacheco moved in political circles and was friends with influential people."

The detective cut in.

"Did he and Marçal get on well?"

Cândido strained his memory.

"I've a feeling they barely even greeted one another."

Del Bosco started circling the room, propelled by a sudden sense of encouragement.

"*Eis aí!* There you have it: they were partners trading precious stones, but to avoid suspicion they feigned mutual indifference. Everything points to the two murders being connected. The gemstones that Marçal offered guests were merely a front, a cover for larger deals. I've already asked the Polícia Federal and Interpol to look into the case."

He stopped walking round the room and said, "Has *senhor* got anything else to add regarding Pacheco?"

"*Não*, we were never friends."

"*Bem*, I appreciate *senhor* coming in."

As he was being shown out of the room, Cândido asked:

"Why did *senhor* insist on Beatriz being questioned?"

"Couldn't the killer have gained access to the hotel through her?" said Del Bosco. Seeing Cândido's look of disapproval, he added, "I have to follow up every hypothesis."

Cândido turned to face the detective.

"And, in such a hypothesis, who gave the killer access to the hotel when Seu Marçal was murdered and we didn't even know the girl existed?"

"Jorge," said the detective.

"Jorge?!" exclaimed Cândido. "The man *senhor* arrested without any evidence and paraded before the public as the 'Lapa Decapa'?"

Del Bosco smiled, unamused.

"As I've already said, out of fear, Jorge confessed to a crime he did not commit."

INTERLUDE

"Come on, man, have the guts to say what you really think," said Odidnac.

"If you insist, I'll go for it."

A SUSPICION

"Was it fear that led Jorge to confess to a crime he didn't commit, or was it certain police methods?" asked Cândido. "If it weren't for an identical crime having been committed, he'd now be appearing before a jury and facing a life in prison."

"Thanks for coming in," said Del Bosco.

Cândido stepped through the door. Then he turned and suddenly gave voice to what was bothering him.

"*Senhor* asked me if I thought the killer was someone from inside the hotel. I gave my verdict resident by resident, suspect by suspect. However, it wouldn't surprise me in the least if the killer turned out to be someone from inside the police."

The *delegado* didn't like what he'd heard, but he didn't react. He knew Cândido was upset.

PERVERTS

"Dona Dinó," said Del Bosco, looking troubled, "the moral integrity of *senhora*'s hotel is in ruins. How does *senhora* think the killer got in without leaving any clues?"

The landlady thrust her hands under Osíris's back legs, picked him up and placed him on her right shoulder. Osíris made himself comfortable, moulding to the shape of Dona Dinó's body.

"Doutor Pacheco's death doesn't really surprise me," she said. "He always hung about with big-shot contractors and politicians. I never said anything, but there was one thing I could never understand: why did he live at the hotel if he was so well connected? I can understand why Larência and Rosaura live in an economical guest house in Lapa. Same with Diamante Negro. In another environment he might suffer prejudice. Professor Cândido is accustomed to a simple lifestyle. I can see why he feels at home under my roof. And Marcelo prefers saving on rent what he can spend on drink. But Pacheco?! He was no king, yet he acted like royalty. Unless it was all an act. I suppose we'll soon find out if all that grandstanding was cover for some unsavoury business."

"And what unsavoury business does *senhora* think he could have been involved in?" asked the detective, pleased to see a witness opening up for a change.

"I never mistrusted Marçal," Dona Dinó went on, ignoring the question. "But after these two tragedies, I'm no longer so sure. Were his frequent disappearances really trips to Minas?"

Del Bosco interrupted her.

"I went up to Vale do Rio Doce and confirmed he went there regularly, bought gemstones and amused himself with *putas*."

"*Ora, senhor*," said Dona Dinó. She moved the cat on to her left shoulder. "If Marçal and Pacheco had one thing in common, it was that they were both perverts."

"Perverts?!" the detective said, surprised.

"*Sim*," Dona Dinó confirmed. "Marçal couldn't look at a girl's legs without getting all smutty. Pacheco was caught sneaking into Rosaura's room only the other night. I had to reprimand him and remind him of the rules."

Del Bosco leaned back on the hind legs of his chair and rested his knees on the edge of the table.

"Is there a drop of morality anywhere among *senhora*'s guests?"

Dona Dinó put the cat down in her lap.

"*Ora*, do I look like the sort of woman who pries into people's affairs? What they get up to in their private lives is their own business. As long as they don't bring it into the hotel."

"*Obrigado*, Dona Dinó," said the detective. "*Senhora* has helped me more than she can imagine."

"Perverts…" Del Bosco whispered through his teeth, as he closed the door behind the old lady.

THE SIEGE

"Tell me about Doutor Pacheco trying to rape you," said the detective.

Rosaura recounted the episode. When she'd finished, Del Bosco regarded her thoughtfully.

"Did you tell anyone outside the hotel about what happened?"

"*Não*, no one," Rosaura lied. "I was too ashamed."

Rosaura had actually told everyone at the mansion where she worked, in order to justify her lateness, but she didn't want her employers mixed up in the murky goings-on at Hotel Brasil.

"Didn't you tell your family in Goiás? Maybe you mentioned it in a letter?" the detective persisted. "Perhaps you spilled your heart out to one of your *amigas*, or to a boyfriend?"

"*Não, senhor.* My family saw the beheadings on TV and were worried about me. Imagine if I then told them I'd been assaulted!"

Del Bosco was convinced the girl was hiding something. Her behaviour was different to when he'd questioned her before. This time she replied with more poise, as if she'd been practising.

"In your previous statement, you said Pacheco stared at your legs a lot," said Del Bosco, staring at the legs in question. They were crossed, knees poking out from underneath the hem of her skirt. "Would you say that Pacheco and Marçal were perverts?"

Rosaura uncrossed her legs, tugging at her skirt and trying to cover up her knees.

"There are all sorts of people in this world, *senhor.* Whether Pacheco and Marçal were or weren't perverts, *não sei.* But I will say this: they had it coming. Folk don't get killed like that unless it's payback for a debt of some sort."

"Let's get to the heart of the matter," said Del Bosco. He stood up and sat down on the edge of the table, very close to Rosaura. "The debt was with you. They tried to rape you and you arranged for someone to cut off their sick heads. Thanks to your help, the killer got in and out of the hotel without leaving a trace."

Rosaura stared at him, wide-eyed. Her face went from white to pink to red. She plunged her head into her hands and bent forward, sobbing uncontrollably.

POSES

"Is *senhora* familiar with this collection of magazines?" the detective said challengingly, as he spread them out over the table. Madame Larência sat before him. She was concerned to have been called in for further questioning. The magazines contained naked women in pornographic poses.

"I imagine *senhor* flicks through magazines about guns and police stories. In much the same way, I'm familiar with this type of magazine. It's part of my job. Almost all the *meninas* I represent pose for photos."

"*Sim,* but don't these particular publications belong to *senhora*?" he said. He handed Madame Larência a magazine.

She glanced at the cover, then placed the magazine back on the table.

"I don't know where *senhor* is going with this," she muttered uncomfortably. "But these magazines aren't mine, my dear. I don't collect magazines. I don't collect anything, not even regrets."

"And this?" Del Bosco produced his next exhibit. "Is this not *senhora's*?"

Madame Larência recognized her own business card.

"*Bem,* obviously it is, *senhor.* Unless there's someone else with the exact same name and address as me."

"This card, *senhora,* was found inside one of these magazines," said the detective. He raised the tone of his voice, attempting to intimidate her. "And these magazines were found inside Doutor Pacheco's room."

"*Ora,*" said Madame Larência, fighting back but unable to hide her nervousness, "what fault is it of mine, *senhor,* if Pacheco mixed my business card in with his dirty magazines? I gave him my card just like I give it to any man who asks me to find him companions."

Del Bosco became animated.

"Does *senhora* mean to say she admits soliciting *garotas* for Pacheco?"

Madame Larência held her bag tightly to her chest in an act of comfort.

"As a *delegado*, I'm sure *senhor* knows very well how these things work. Pacheco moved in political circles. From time to time he asked me to find a girl to escort a *deputado* on a trip, or to keep a *ministro* company while he was in Rio. I found the girls; he passed them on."

"And how did you split the *grana*?" asked Del Bosco.

"I don't think he earned any money out of it. The client paid the girl, who in turn paid me a commission. Pacheco probably got some kind of job security out of knowing about the private lives of important people."

"And how many women did *senhora* arrange for Seu Marçal?"

The colour drained from Madame Larência's cheeks, highlighting her wrinkles. Her fingers tightened their grip on the straps of her handbag. They trembled slightly.

"I never arranged any girls for Marçal. He never asked me to and I never offered."

"But *senhora* knew he was a pervert?"

"*Pelo amor de Deus*, Marçal was my friend, *senhor*! There was never a hint of sex between us."

BODY AND SPIRIT

The pink three-piece suit Diamante Negro wore to the police station left Del Bosco in some doubt.

"Is that outfit supposed to be formal or provocative?" he asked.

"Oh, *delegado*, now is not the time to make fun of me. I'm scared half to death of becoming the next victim. I can even picture the headlines: 'Transvestite decapitated in Lapa!' *Ai, meu Deus*, these media types are so ignorant they don't even know the difference between a tranny and a *transformista*."

"It's precisely so you don't run the risk of being the next victim that we need to move this investigation along as quickly as possible," the detective said.

"*Senhor*, I wish I could help, I really do," said Diamante Negro, "but this whole business is turning my head upside down."

"Careful," said Del Bosco, "it might fall off."

"*Pelo amor de Deus, senhor!* Stop teasing!"

"Do you think someone at the hotel is mixed up in this?" asked the detective.

"*Não sei.* There are eccentrics to suit all tastes at the hotel, *senhor*. But could any of them have attacked a big *cabra* like Seu Marçal and caused all that mayhem without anyone hearing a thing? Could any of them have set upon Pacheco without him... Now, how would he have put it? *Ah, já sei...* 'categorically denying it'?" said Diamante Negro. He adopted a deep voice in imitation of the political aide.

"Nobody attacked or set upon anyone," said the detective. "There were no signs of struggle between the killer and either of the victims."

Diamante Negro held his hands up, the fingers spread wide.

"*Senhor*, I've already had *cinco – um, dois, três, quatro, cinco* – locks fitted on my door! It would take a bazooka and a tank to get in."

"In your opinion," said Del Bosco, "were Marçal and Pacheco perverts?"

"Perverts?!" Diamante said, surprised. "*Ora*, who knows?" He stroked his beardless chin with his thin fingers. "Seu

Marçal loved *meninas*, and Pacheco wasn't exactly backward in coming forward – just ask Rosaura. But to go from that to crowning them perverts, *senhor*, is to take a leap as big as the one between my male body and my female spirit."

TEMPERAMENTS

"So, Del Bosco, who's next to have a confession beaten out of them?" said Marcelo, as he entered the detective's room.

"Rest assured, it won't be you," replied the *delegado* with a sense of discomfort he couldn't quite hide. "But I do aim to clear the murders up very soon. Aren't you scared your head might be next?"

"I get off my head every night," said Marcelo. He plucked a cigarette out of a packet in his shirt pocket. "The way things are going, the next head to roll will be yours. I interviewed the Secretário de Segurança yesterday. He told me, off the record, that if you don't catch the 'Lapa Decapa' in the next few days, he's taking you off the case and putting a new team in place."

Del Bosco adjusted his collar, as if checking his neck was still intact.

"Do you think Madame Larência could have plotted these murders?"

"Madame Larência?!" said Marcelo, astonished.

The detective sought to capitalize on his confusion.

"And Rosaura?"

"Larência and Rosaura? Now if you'd told me you suspected Diamante Negro, I wouldn't have been at all surprised: gays can be very temperamental, mood swings over the slightest thing. But, Larência and Rosaura..." said Marcelo. "I know you'd rather not hear it, but my newspaper is planning a probe into whether the police are mixed up in this. They usually are in crimes with no suspects."

The detective gave a strained smile.

"Marcelo, I won't lie to you; not all policemen are saints. I know colleagues who practise extortion and pimping, others who run protection rackets for drug-traffickers and *jogo do bicho* chiefs. But playing at serial killers is not our game. This is the work of a *maluco*."

UNDER SUSPICION

After questioning all the Hotel Brasil residents, Delegado Del Bosco ordered that two suspects be remanded in custody: Rosaura Dorotéia dos Santos and Madame Larência. The former, the police report stated, because she'd quarrelled with the victim and could conceivably have plotted the murder to avenge his trying to rape her. The latter because the police had uncovered a large collection of pornographic material in Doutor Pacheco's room and the *cafetina*'s business card had been found in among it.

Yet something still nagged at the detective: was it definitely the same killer, or could the same method have been used to mislead the police?

COVER

"Does *senhor* know what he's let himself in for with this girl?" said Del Bosco, welcoming Cândido back to the police station. "She has a bounty on her head."

"What does *senhor* suggest I do?" said Cândido. "Hand her back in to a young offenders' institute?"

"That would resolve *senhor*'s situation but rather complicate hers," the detective admitted. "If she falls into police hands, sooner or later someone's going to settle a score with her. It makes more sense to keep her out of circulation."

"Why is *senhor* suddenly so interested in her welfare?" said Cândido, starting to get worried.

"I could tell she wasn't the typical drug-addict *moleque*, born to be a *bandido*. She's very fond of *senhor*, and I think it would be best for all concerned if she remained under *senhor*'s care. If I hear of any specific threat, I'll let *senhor* know," said Del Bosco.

Cândido explained the situation to Mônica, who agreed to help until he found somewhere else for Beatriz to go.

INTERLUDE

"Odid, this torch in my heart grows bigger by the day. Soon it will be a giant bonfire. Even worrying about Bia doesn't provide any respite from my fixation with Mônica."

"Is it stronger than what you felt for Cibele?"

"With Cibele perhaps I experienced the awakening of love, for I did feel a great warmth inside me. But it was like eating chocolate: a warm feeling that soon turned to thirst."

"Not like with Ângela, then?"

"With Ângela I sampled the glorification of the flesh, dizzy attraction, ecstasy exploding."

"What's so different this time?"

"This time I'm savouring the bittersweet taste of love. I'm going round and round in circles, powerlessly, confusingly, revolving

around someone whose face is the door to a world that is real and yet woven from dreams."

"Why don't you tell her this?"

"I fear she already knows and that my dizzy feelings are not reciprocated. I've never seen her looking at me the way I look at her. Though we do worry about Bia in much the same way… I see Mônica even when we're apart, I can guess her movements. I'd give anything to know once and for all what she thinks of me."

CLARIFICATION

Dear Cândido,

Your presence within me, so tender and endearing, assumes proportions that make me sure I'm in love. I don't want to upset you, put you in an uncomfortable position or prey upon your deepest emotions. Above all else, I can't stand the thought of losing you as a friend. But I feel drunk at the mere mention of your name. Just knowing you exist activates my most vital energies.

I love you!

Mônica

9   *Taco*

There was a birthday cake the size of a Ferris wheel in the middle of an open field. It had a chocolate coating and was covered in small yellow-and-green candles. The day was very hot and the sun was melting the chocolate, sending it dribbling down the cake, over layers of nuts and cream, to the ground, where it made furrows in the earth and formed sweet rivers of vanilla-scented lava that set off for the sea.

The dream dissolved as Cândido heard a broom handle tapping against his door. He tried to recover the scene. All he could recall was that it was some sort of commemoration, for whom or for what he could not say. Fragments of memory remained like dark silhouettes, leaving a bitter taste in his mouth.

He put his dressing gown on and opened the door. Dona Dinó stood there with a look of concern on her face.

"Senhor Chico Lima just called. He said *senhor* is to phone him right away."

Cândido splashed some water on his face, got dressed and went out to the phone in the dining room. Dona Dinó was sitting at the table by the window, broom pressed to her chest, Osíris asleep at her feet. Her eyes fixed themselves on the phone while he spoke. She directed a strange energy at the mouthpiece, as if she could see the person at the other end of the line.

Chico Lima told Cândido that Taco was being taken to a juvenile correction facility on a *fazenda* somewhere in the Rio state interior. But the police had ordered that he first take part in a crime scene reconstruction before the juvenile court judge.

"It's scheduled for midday today," said Chico Lima. "I think we should be there."

PREMONITION

Cândido bid Dona Dinó farewell, but found his path blocked by the broom: she'd let it slip from her hands and fall at his feet. She swooped down and picked it up, in one swift motion.

"*Senhor* should think twice about going to certain places today," she said in a premonitory tone. "May God protect *senhor.*"

The warning intrigued him.

"How so, Dona Dinó?"

"Forgive me," she said. "I have no right to interfere in *senhor*'s affairs."

"Don't say that! *Senhora* is like a second mother to me," he said, leaving her visibly touched. "But don't worry, my *santo* is strong."

THE ANGRY MOB

When he got to the *favela*, Cândido saw that a number of onlookers had already gathered, attracted by the presence of police and press vehicles. A green-and-yellow rope cordoned off the area around the *barraco* where the old lady had been killed by her drugged-up grandson. There was no sign of Taco yet. The crowd behind the rope was starting to get agitated.

The police authorities knew Chico Lima, and he and Cândido were allowed inside the segregated area. They took a quick look inside the *barraco*, a one-room hut made of clapboard, cardboard and corrugated iron. It had been built precariously close to a cesspit, Taco and his grandma sharing the space with rats and cockroaches from a sewage pipe. The walls inside the hut were adorned with photos of actors and actresses cut out from magazines, as well as a print of São Jorge on his white horse, sticking a spear into the flaming jaws of a dragon.

Taco arrived when the sun was at its apex. He came in a police car, accompanied by the Juiz de Menores and the *delegado* in charge of the case. The boy's white reformatory uniform and yellow plastic flip-flops contrasted with the blackness of his skin.

His look of fear subsided as he recognized a few faces in the crowd, but as he was led over to the *barraco* by the judge and the detective, someone shouted:

"Lynch him!"

Others picked up on the cry and the refrain quickly spread, moving through the throng like a ripple on a lake. Taco became increasingly frightened. He huddled close to the judge for protection.

"Lynch him! Lynch him!" roared the mob, rocking back and forth behind the cordon.

Cândido and Chico Lima urged everyone to calm down and not compromise the judge's work, but their words reached only a handful of people at the front. The police started to worry about the level of unrest and tried to reinforce the barrier they'd formed around Taco and the two officials. The detective suggested they get back in the car.

Three young men broke through the cordon and advanced aggressively on Taco. The police raised their truncheons. One of the young men was struck across the back. Another officer pulled out a gun and pointed it at the three aggressors. A circle of police tried to escort the judge and Taco back to the car, the judge wrapping his arms around the boy, who was now crying convulsively. Women grabbed at the policemen's clothes, tearing fabric and scratching skin. Reporters wavered between registering the facts and helping to contain the crowd's temper, until their cameras were snatched off them and thrown through the air, then fought over as booty on the ground.

The three interlopers lunged at Taco. One of them got hold of an arm. Panic-stricken, Taco begged the judge and detective not to abandon him. Truncheons swung freely. The angry mob grew in size and rage, possessed by a rabid fury.

Pressed up against the *barraco*, Cândido and Chico Lima continued to appeal for calm. Their calls fell on deaf ears. The *delegado* took out his gun and fired two shots in the air. Taco's attackers let go of him and the *delegado* told the *juiz* to take the boy inside the *barraco* and wait until backup came.

The judge, Taco and a police guard waded through the crowd, as if in slow motion, pushing and shoving to open a path to the *barraco*. The atmosphere turned hostile again: a hail of punches, spit and stones rained down on them.

Cândido watched, trapped in a corner, wincing every time their progress was halted and they were forced backwards. He said a silent prayer, hoped for a miracle. Unless police reinforcements arrived soon, a tragedy would be inevitable.

Men armed with iron bars suddenly appeared, fighting their way through to Taco.

"Kill him! Kill him!" the crowd chanted in unison.

The men seized Taco. His screaming ceased as a metal bar split his skull. Blood flew everywhere, splattering the face of a boy tying the rope cordon round Taco's neck. Taco fell. A cavalcade of stamping feet passed over his body.

Sirens were heard and the mob quickly dispersed, like ants surprised by a gush of water in a sugar bowl.

Taco's remains lay mixed in with the mud and slops. All that could really be distinguished was the green-and-yellow chord he'd been strangled with.

10   *Revelation*

INTERLUDE

"Odid, last night I dreamed of Mônica."

"There you go, man: proof she inhabits your subconscious. What was the dream like?"

"There was a lake. The side of the lake fell into a crystal waterfall. She was swimming at the bottom, naked. I approached from the side of a mountain, wearing crampons and dressed as an alpine hiker. When she saw me, she tried to protect her modesty by hiding behind the veil of water. But it was hopeless. The closer I got, the more she laughed. I moved towards her, and, as the water poured down on me, my clothes came off, too, until I was naked except for my boots, wet and heavy on my feet."

"And then you embraced?" said Odidnac.

"That was my intention. But when I opened my arms, she laughed and her body started moving up the sheet of water, pulled by an invisible hand. She went higher and higher, further and further away from me, and then disappeared over the top of the waterfall."

"How do you feel now, man?"

"Full of longing. Longing for the future."

GALLANTRY

Rosaura and Madame Larência were released due to lack of evidence. While they were in jail together, the *cafetina* tried to lure the housemaid into her fold.

"You don't even actually have to go into battle, my dear," said Madame Larência. "Get paid up front, distract the client with idle chit-chat and get him drunk. Then when H-hour comes, let slip that you had some tests last month because you were worried you'd got a venereal disease. They're all terrified of Aids."

But Rosaura seemed more interested in Olinto Del Bosco's gallantry. He regularly came to fetch her from the cells and let her sit in his office watching police films.

DISAPPEARANCE

Beatriz disappeared again during Carnival. Cândido thought that Delegado Del Bosco must have shopped her, but he got a call from Dona Dinó on Shrove Tuesday and was forced to admit his suspicions had been unfounded.

"The girl phoned to say she's fine. *Senhor* is not to worry and she'll be back in a few weeks."

THE DEAL

One morning, when Cândido had left for the publisher's, Beatriz waited until Dona Dinó was distracted, then slipped out. She wandered about the city centre and hung out with a gang of kids on the steps of the Theatro Municipal. They were sniffing glue, but she turned it down when offered some. She begged for a snack from a lady stuffing her face with *pastéis* in the Edifício Avenida Central shopping arcade and the woman bought her a drink and a hot dog, more out of fear than kindness. Then Beatriz took off and headed towards Central do Brasil station.

As night fell, she mixed in with carnival performers outside the *sambódromo*. She was watching a samba school warming up bodies and tambourines for the parade, when she saw a familiar face in the crowd. She went straight over and hugged him from behind, covering his eyes with her hands:

"Guess who and win a prize."

He flinched, took hold of her hands and exclaimed, "Bia!"

"Bola!" she cried, giving him a big hug.

"Wow! Great to see you, *garota*!"

He looked different. He was thinner, his eyes were deeper-set and his teeth had yellowed with nicotine. His limbs had lengthened and his movement had become more agile: there was little of the awkwardness and innocence that had previously defined him. She saw he was no longer a boy. She also saw he was dressed in smart clothes and had an expensive wristwatch.

"Where've you been hiding?" he asked.

"Around," she answered evasively. Then she laughed, adding, "but now it's all *tudo bem*."

"I play for the Pavão-Pavãozinho *favela* these days," said Bola. "My game has won the trust of the guys with the *grana*."

"So I see, *malandro*," she teased. "A career man now."

Bola took her by the hand.

"Let's go and talk over there."

233

Bola couldn't believe his luck. His ex-girlfriend had landed in his lap like a gift from heaven. One deal would be enough to get her on board.

Beatriz was surprised by the way she reacted to seeing Bola again. Feelings that had lain dormant suddenly stirred. When he took her by the hand and led her away from the samba schools, the woman taking shape inside her started doing somersaults. A warm sense of security turned into one of complicity, and before she knew it she was gripped by attraction.

Up against the Cemitério do Caju wall, the stony eyes of a marble angel looking down on them, Bola kissed Beatriz on the lips and hungrily ran his hands over her anxious body.

As she lay back naked on a gravestone, Beatriz smiled at the brightness of the stars that seemed to twinkle only for her, while Bola moved his body to the agonizing beat of the *cuica* drums coming from the *sambódromo*. His eyes ran over an epitaph behind Beatriz's head, an apparent jumble of nonsense words: *Fama fumus, homo humus, finis cinis?*

MULE

Beatriz got to Foz do Iguaçu on Ash Wednesday, in a truck laden with sacks of cement. They crossed the border into Paraguay, she pretending to be the truck-driver's daughter, and unloaded the merchandise. At an import emporium, the driver filled the truck back up with boxes of Chinese plastic knick-knacks – toys, cups, stationery – destined for fixed-price discount stores in Brazil.

As they were leaving, the manager of the emporium gave

the truck-driver's "daughter" a present: a teddy bear almost as big as she was.

Customs inspectors stopped the vehicle at the border back into Brazil. The driver showed them his documents and tax receipts and let them examine his load.

The inspectors soon waved the truck through, paying no attention to the girl hugging the bear with enough cocaine in its belly to keep the Pavão-Pavãozinho *favela* dealing for a month.

INTERLUDE

"Odid, I fear losing Mônica. I don't know whether jealousy is getting the better of me or whether Bramante really is interested in her, but whenever she walks in the room he gets as excited as I do. It's as if her presence soothes an itch in our souls. She rejuvenates us."

"You need to find out what you mean to her," said Odidnac.

"She's not stupid. She knows we're both in thrall to her, but while she does her best to avoid Bramante, she's warm and kind to me. Am I destined for ever to be the trusted friend, or have I got what it takes to be her man?"

"Why don't you ask her?" said Odidnac.

"Every night I convince myself that I'll open up to her in the morning. But then I lose courage as soon as I see her. I fear getting a loud and resounding não. *Yet I know that if you never take a chance in life you get eaten up from the outside, like a hot bowl of* mingau. *It's terrible to think that my own insecurities might stop her liking me."*

"Or is this just the self-delusion of a lovesick heart?" said Odidnac.

"Meu Deus, how it hurts suffering for love! Especially when you know the only cure is love itself! Time eases the suffering, and can even make it go away. But what time can't heal is the wound."

DECLARATION

"Now I accept," said Cândido as he walked through the door. Mônica had invited him over for dinner and promised to cook *camarões à la provençal*, to rid him of his false impression.

"Accept what?" said Mônica, smiling.

"That drink you offered me last time I was here, that I never got to taste."

Mônica gave him a warm hug.

"And there was something you were going to tell me that I never got to hear."

"Something I was going to tell you? I thought you were the one who had something to tell me," said Cândido, returning her hug and kissing her on the cheek with a vigour that surprised himself.

"OK, but there's something important I have to do first," said Mônica, removing herself from his grasp. She took his face in both hands and kissed him on the lips. Cândido felt as if he could walk on hot coals.

He opened a bottle of *vinho branco* and offered to help in the kitchen.

While Mônica cleaned the shrimp and marinated them in salt and orange juice, Cândido chopped up the garlic so fine it was as if he was trying to split atoms. She put the rice on to boil, adding nothing by way of seasoning, but lining the bottom of the pan with extra virgin olive oil. As she did so, a satisfying feeling came over her. Cândido was no lord of the manor, sitting in the lounge with a drink, eyes glued to the TV, waiting for the missus to make him his dinner. Cândido was a companion who stood by her side and breathed in the aroma of the garlic as it turned light blond in the hot oil, ready to be poured over the shrimp.

He added a few splashes of *molho de pimenta* to the *camarões*, while she drizzled olive oil over the side salad.

As the rice cooked on the hob and the prawns baked in the oven, Mônica and Cândido sat on footstools, glasses of *vinho* in their hands. They conducted a conversation in which their eyes said more than their words and feelings flowed with greater strength than their thoughts.

When the food was ready, they tipped the pan of rice over the shrimp, added a little parsley and gave everything a good stir. They took the dish into the lounge, where the table lay beautifully set and candlelit.

"What have you got to tell me, then?" said Mônica, as she opened a linen napkin over her lap.

"It's already been said with that kiss, *meu amor*," replied Cândido. "Do you still have something to tell me?"

Mônica thought for a moment.

"Hold on," she said, and stood up. "I've got something to give you."

She went into the bedroom, opened the drawer to the bedside table and came back clutching a bundle of letters.

"There you go," she said, handing them to Cândido and sitting back down.

"What are they?" he asked, intrigued.

"Love letters I wrote to you but never had the courage to send."

"If you don't mind," said Cândido, "I'd like to read them later, when I get back to the hotel. That way, you'll be by my side."

"Take them with you. I don't want you sitting here reading them now."

"So, everything you have to say is written here?" said Cândido, patting the letters with his hand.

Mônica frowned as she served up the food. Then she stopped and winced.

"What I really want to tell you, I seem unable to write down. Remember when you said you wanted to go to Itaguaí to look for Beatriz?"

"*Sim.* I thought she might have gone back to where she'd grown up. What about it?"

Mônica put her elbows on the table and held her head in her hands. She looked up and stared straight at Cândido.

"If we're going to start a relationship, there are certain aspects of our lives we have to reveal to one another. I like things plain and straight, *chocolate à espanhola.* So listen carefully. When I was at university, I took part in student protests against the dictatorship. I didn't belong to any particular faction of the left, I was just angry at the way the generals interfered with education. A march was arranged one Friday afternoon, going right through the centre of town and up to the obelisk on Avenida Beira-Mar. To outmanoeuvre the police, a special tactic was devised whereby protesters assembled in groups of five. The idea was that five people on their own wouldn't arouse suspicion as they looked like passers-by, but then forty groups of five would merge together outside Igreja de Candelária and march as one down Avenida Rio Branco. They'd be joined by more groups of five at every junction, so if the police blocked the march off after one hundred or two hundred yards, a new wave of protesters would surge in behind them. I agreed to be part of a group of five that met on the corner of Avenida Rio Branco and Rua do Ouvidor. We set off like a human ant trail down the street. The police chose not to intervene and the march grew thicker as it made its way towards the obelisk. Everyone chanted protest slogans and we unveiled banners above our heads. I was wearing a Che Guevara T-shirt and joined in enthusiastically with a chorus of '*Abaixo a ditadura!*' A protester came up to me outside Edifício Avenida Central and said, 'I feel sick, I think I'm going to faint.' She was about the same age as me and held her hand to her forehead. 'Would you mind helping me get to a bathroom? I need some water.' We went into the shopping arcade at the bottom of the building and down the escalators. I asked a man where the toilets were and he pointed to a bar at the back. When we got to the entrance of the bar, we were suddenly surrounded. I never found out whether they were police, military or paramilitaries. 'You're under arrest!' a guy in a black leather jacket said. I started trembling with fear and tried to explain myself. The girl who'd asked for help had vanished. Doubtless she was bait and had gone back up to pull the same trick on another protester. The bar had been converted into a temporary prison. It was full of students. After a little while, I was taken out through the back, into Largo da Carioca, where I was put in a car with two men. One of them ran his hand over my body in a way that made me very uncomfortable. He asked me if I was carrying a gun. Then they blindfolded me with some kind of special dark glasses. The car set off in the direction of Praça Tiradentes. I tried to memorize the route and I managed up to a certain point, until fear got the better of me. Eventually I heard the sound of an iron gate opening and closing and I realized we'd gone into a garage or yard. I was taken out of the car and led into a building. A woman's voice shouted at me: 'Take those glasses off!' She was old enough to be my mother. Her face was like a mask, round and white, with narrow eyes devoid of all expression. She was sitting on a chair behind a table and there was nothing else in the room, no other furniture except a dirty mattress chucked on the floor in a corner. I noticed there were no windows. '*Documentos*!' said the woman. I told her that all I'd taken to the march were the clothes on my back. The woman took a ballpoint pen out and leaned over the table. 'Personal details, then.' She asked me my name and so forth and wrote my answers down on a sheet of yellow paper. 'Do you know the student leaders?' she asked. I barely managed to make my voice heard. '*Não*, I'm not affiliated to any group or political party.' 'I'm not asking you if you're affiliated to terrorist groups!' yelled the woman. 'I asked if you know the student leaders.' She opened a file and showed me a photo of a boy. 'What about him?' 'I've never seen him before in my life,' I said, honestly. The woman stood up and approached me menacingly. 'Mônica, we know for a fact that you're Alexandre's lover, so the sooner you tell us where he's hiding, the better.' '*Pelo amor de Deus*,' I said, 'I swear I've never heard of the guy – I haven't even got a boyfriend.' The woman pinched me hard on the arm. I yelped in pain. 'That's just for starters,' she said. 'I'd refresh your memory quick smart if I were you. Tell me where Alexandre is now or I'll hand you over to Paranhão – he just loves playing with little dolls like you.' I began to whimper as cold shivers ran through me. The woman slapped me in the face. 'Stop your wailing! Where is Alexandre hiding?' I told her over and over again, through floods of tears, that I knew no one called Alexandre.

240

'*Senhora* must have the wrong Mônica,' I said, but the woman shouted abuse at me and said she'd soon jog my memory. 'Take your clothes off!' she demanded. I took off my top and trousers, shaking uncontrollably and feeling my limbs stiffen as I did so. The woman came over and yanked away my bra. 'Take off your knickers!' she yelled. I was left totally naked, stricken with panic. I knelt on the floor and started to pray out loud. The woman bent down and squeezed one of my nipples. 'For the last time: where is Alexandre hiding?' She didn't even wait for an answer. She pushed me over, stood up and kicked me just above the kidneys. I curled myself into a ball and pleaded to God to let me die rather than suffer. '*Bem*,' said the woman, opening the door. 'As you refuse to collaborate, I'll leave you in Paranhão's capable hands.' As she left, a huge man walked in, tremendously fat. All he had on was a pair of swimming trunks. He came over to me, walking like a bear, smiling mockingly. He grabbed me by the arm and dragged me over to the mattress. 'OK then, *beleza*, I'm going to make you come until you scream where Alexandre's hiding.' I tried to fight him off, I begged him to leave me alone, but he held me firmly by the wrists and pinned me down on the mattress. I was horrified but I went on fighting and kicking, until the man took off his trunks and slapped me so hard I passed out. When I woke, I was alone in the room. I was cold, my vagina burned and bled and my body was covered in cuts and bruises. I banged on the door but nobody came. I was left there until the following morning, when the woman reappeared. She gave me back my clothes and said, 'Get dressed. You're not the Mônica we're looking for.' I was put back in the car; my eyes were covered with the dark glasses again. They drove me to a petrol station in Aterro do Flamengo and pushed me out."

241

FRUIT

There was a prolonged silence after Mônica had finished telling the story. They both stared at their hands as their fingers nervously arranged and rearranged the cutlery on the tablecloth.

"I'd always thought the torture stories were exaggerations of the left," Cândido murmured. "I was a humanities student at the time, at a college deep in the Minas interior. We were given the impression the military had saved Brazil from the communist threat. It was only later I found out that behind the facade of tranquility were prisoners, exiles, disappearances and deaths."

"Two months later," Mônica went on, "I went to see a gynaecologist to find out whether the trauma justified my period being late. I found out I was pregnant. I was put under a lot of pressure to abort, but I decided to have the child. I couldn't face submitting my body to further violence. But nor did I feel capable of raising a child I'd not planned for. I had a girl," she said, staring straight at Cândido.

He stared back at her, saw that her face was starting to relax. They began eating: cold crustaceans.

"I was young," she said. "I didn't have the resources to look after a baby, and I lacked the subjectivity and single-mindedness a mother needs to raise an unexpected child. Before she was even a month old, I gave the baby girl to a public orphanage. I was told no more about her, nor ever felt the need to know. But since meeting Bia, I've thought about my daughter a lot. At first, Bia's presence made me uncomfortable. It reminded me of my baby. But gradually, Bia won me round."

Cândido raised his glass to his lips and savoured the way the wine moistened his tongue. He looked at Mônica with tender eyes.

"Do you want to try and find your daughter?"

"*Não*. That page of my life has turned, though I do remember her in my prayers. What I want is to find Bia."

"Mônica, if Bia reappears," said Cândido, "I'd really like to adopt her, me and you. What do you think?"

Mônica's eyes welled up. She smiled.

"It was that very certainty, Cândido, that awoke my love for you."

For dessert, they went to bed.

11 *Nuptials*

"Mônica Kundali, do you accept Cândido Oliveira to be your lawfully wedded husband?" asked the priest. He was a fat friar with a red face, small hands and chubby fingers.

"I do," said the bride.

Mônica was wearing a long, silky crêpe dress and had a fascinator of pink flowers in her hair. She was trying hard to hold back the tears, not wanting her make-up to run.

Next it was the groom's turn to give his consent. Cândido was overjoyed, except for one tiny detail: Beatriz was still missing.

The congregation was packed full of the bride's and groom's friends and family. Dona Dinó had arrived wearing a yellow pleated dress, arm in arm with Diamante Negro. The *transformista* drew everyone's attention in a bright-red top hat and tails with purple velvet collar and cuffs. Rosaura wore white and leaned shyly against Madame Larência, whose face was covered in an especially thick coat of cosmetics. Marcelo wore jeans and trainers in a lone protest against social convention.

The Igreja do Outeiro da Glória was too small for so many guests and not everyone could fit in the church. Yet those left outside were not too distraught: it was a hot Saturday afternoon and it was quite a relief not to be sitting inside the stuffy church.

Bramante was neither inside nor out: he'd chosen not to attend, though he did send the happy couple a set of bone-china plates as a gift.

The priest launched into a sermon exalting conjugal faithfulness, prompting Diamante Negro to whisper to Dona Dinó, "*Heim!* Most of us aren't even faithful to ourselves, let alone others!"

The priest then preached against abortion, as if programmed to do so regardless of his audience. He stressed his personal friendship with the groom and praised the bride's intellectual background, all in a muddle of uninspiring words and Latin quotations devoid of anything remotely transcendental.

What caught Rosaura's attention was that not once did he utter the word love.

Dona Dinó admired the elegant women and dashing men, while Madame Larência was reduced to tears by the Gregorian chant underscoring the ceremony, causing her make-up to smudge.

THE RECEPTION

Lassale threw a barbecue for the bride and groom at his house in Barra da Tijuca. The garden was thick with the smell of grilled meat. In one corner, a group of publishers had a whisky-fuelled discussion about the book trade. The general consensus was that things were not going well. Paper had become more expensive, the government had cut back on its purchases of educational material, distributors were demanding a bigger slice of the pie and *livrarias* were closing down in the face of the recession.

Several of the publishers admitted they'd have been bankrupt themselves if it hadn't been for self-help books and crude religious texts, both of which targeted the reader's emotion rather than their reason.

"The important thing," said the host of the party, speaking with the authority of someone who'd scored a modest success with the first instalment of the *Terceiro Milênio* series, "is to steer clear of theology and avoid all doctrine of any known religious persuasion. Fill the books with metaphors, mix different spiritual sources and never make the reader feel guilty with notions of sin. Cut any words that might need looking up in a dictionary and add a sprinkling of mystical beings – elves, angels, demons, wizards, that sort of thing. The goal is to turn God into a pop star: well-produced and apolitical, with some dazzling onstage acrobatics and music that has enough melody and rhythm to hide the poverty of its lyrics. In short, lots of noise and zero substance. The public doesn't want to reflect, only to feel."

THE GOOD DAUGHTER RETURNS HOME

A few nights after getting back from their honeymoon, the newlyweds were fast asleep in Mônica's apartment when the phone rang. It was Madame Larência. Beatriz had turned up at Hotel Brasil and was anxiously asking for Cândido.

Cândido got dressed and headed straight to the hotel. He found Madame Larência in the TV lounge watching a programme showcasing the miraculous powers of an evangelical pastor. The *cafetina* said Beatriz had arrived looking exhausted, so she'd fixed the girl some food, had her take a shower and put her to bed.

Cândido was overcome with emotion when he saw Beatriz fast asleep in Madame Larência's bed, snuggled up among lace sheets and cuddly toys. The room looked more like a maiden's chamber than a bawd's bedroom.

"And where's she been all this time?"

"*Ora*, do I look like the sort of person who goes poking her nose into other people's business?" answered Madame Larência.

Cândido took the girl in his arms and carried her into the lounge. He called Mônica and gave her the good news, saying he'd bring Beatriz back in the morning rather than wake the girl up now. He wanted to wait until he could talk to Beatriz in private, to tell her she now had a home to go to. He lay the girl down on the sofa and settled himself on the carpet beside her, with a cushion for a pillow.

THE PRESENT

When he opened his eyes in the morning, Beatriz was gone. In her place was a quartz clock and an envelope, postmarked Assunción. There was a note inside – *To the bride and groom, with lots of love, Bia* – along with a wad of hundred-dollar bills. Four grand in total.

Cândido had just finished counting the money when the girl came out of the toilet by the dining room.

"What's all this?" he asked, waving the banknotes at her.

"First give me a hug and a kiss," she said smiling. "Congratulations on getting married. I've missed you."

She threw herself on him and then whispered in his ear:

"It's a present."

"*Sim*, but where did you get so much money from?"

"Working for Bola."

Cândido got annoyed.

"Working as what? Doing what?"

"If I were rich, *tio*, I'd be called a trader. But as I'm just a poor flip-flop girl, I suppose I'm a *contrabandista*."

Cândido surprised himself by getting cross and giving the girl a firm telling-off. She burst out crying, tears of real feeling.

"You know what I'm going to do with this money?" he said. "Give it to the Casa do Menor. Now, pull yourself together. I've got good news."

REUNION

As they made their way to the flat, Cândido told Beatriz about the decision he and Mônica had made.

When she opened the door and saw Beatriz, Mônica choked up.

"*Querida*," she babbled, as she crouched down and squeezed Beatriz to her chest, tears running down her face and into the girl's hair.

"*Mamãe!*" exclaimed Beatriz, shedding tears of her own.

THE NEXT VICTIM

A few weeks later, Jorge Maldonado was found dead in his broom cupboard at the back of the hotel.

The tragedy proved just how unfounded Delegado Del Bosco's initial allegations had been. After calling for him repeatedly and getting no response, Dona Dinó went to investigate and found Jorge laid out on his bed among his tools and cleaning equipment. He was dressed in his Botafogo shirt and shorts, and his severed head sat between the football boots on his feet. A blue ribbon from his ponytail dangled down at the cut of the neck.

Two dark holes lay where his eyes should have been.

NEW PROJECT

"And how's it going with Beatriz?" Del Bosco asked Cândido, after calling him in for questioning over Jorge Maldonado's murder.

"*Tudo bem.* We managed to reach an understanding with the Juiz de Menores and Mônica and I are now officially Beatriz's parents. She's back in school and getting treatment from a good psychologist. *Graças a Deus* she reappeared."

"Pleased to hear it," said the detective. "She deserves a decent life. And is *senhor* still working at the publisher's?"

"*Sim,* I'm involved in a new project. I'm writing a history of the suburbs."

"I know *senhor* no longer lives at Hotel Brasil," said Del Bosco, "but tell me about Jorge Maldonado."

12   *The Ritual*

Marcelo finished his soup and loosened his tie. He lit a cigarette then stubbed it out, complaining of a headache.

"I know the perfect cure," said Dona Dinó, as she took away his dirty dishes. "Go and lie down and I'll bring you something to take care of it."

The journalist undressed and waited for the water in the shower to warm up. While he soaped himself down, he thought about the interrogation he'd been subjected to that afternoon. He'd lost count of the number of times he'd been summoned to the Delegacia da Lapa. Del Bosco was still insisting that one of the hotel residents was the "Lapa Decapa", or at the very least an accomplice. Which meant Marcelo remained on his list of suspects.

Right from the start, the journalist had chosen attack as the best form of defence. That afternoon he'd reiterated his claim that the killer had to be a police officer. There was no other way of explaining the ease with which the maniac entered the hotel, went into rooms and caused carnage without leaving any clues.

The allegation had so annoyed the detective that the questioning session had descended into a slanging match. Now, under the shower, Marcelo weighed up the pros and cons of writing an exposé on how the "Lapa Decapa" investigation had failed to get off the ground due to police incompetence.

The matter required careful consideration. He knew running a story like that would not only mean Del Bosco being taken off the case but also the end of the detective's career. Marcelo didn't really want to be the cause of that. But as a journalist, and as someone at the heart of the investigation, he felt public patience had reached its limit. A clue had to appear from somewhere.

He dried himself with his Flamengo towel, put his pyjamas on and climbed into bed. He rolled the towel up and laid it across his face, covering his eyes, for he believed that light aggravated his headache. A few minutes later, Dona Dinó knocked gently on the door with the tip of her broom.

"Come in," he called out.

She turned the door handle with her right hand and entered, holding the broom in her left. Osíris stole in artfully through her legs. Marcelo uncovered his face when he felt the cat jump up on the bed.

Dona Dinó settled herself in the armchair by Marcelo's computer.

"As *senhor* knows, I don't believe in medicine," she said. "But if *senhor* will allow me to perform a little hypnosis, I swear he'll never have a headache again."

"What do I have to do?" asked Marcelo, open to any suggestion that might ease the throbbing at his brain and temples.

"Sit up against the headboard and look into Osíris's eyes," she said, picking up the cat and holding it in her hands.

The journalist stared hard into Osíris's eyes while Dona Dinó whispered phrases in a maternal voice, phrases that made Marcelo feel sleepy. She slowly repeated the refrain:

"*Illujanka… Illujanka…*"

They're not eyes, thought Marcelo, they're little suns that slowly expand and turn, rotating, radiating a golden ring of light… The Arles sun in a Van Gogh painting… Golden coins…

Everything went magically yellow. Marcelo was no longer thinking. He didn't even know if his eyes were open or closed. His mind rocked to the sound of Dona Dinó's mysterious commentary, until he sunk into a new state of consciousness, a soft smile on his lips.

Dona Dinó put Osíris down and picked up the broom. Holding it with both hands and laying it flat across her lap, she opened up the handle and pulled out a sword with a fine triangular blade. She then unscrewed the brush and took out a dagger. She stood up and went over to the man lying in a hypnotic trance. With a firm hand, she thrust the dagger into his heart. He spluttered, his feet flailing about on the mattress and his arms reaching out for the old woman. She covered his face with a pillow and then stabbed him a second time until he stopped moving. He was dead.

Using the tip of the dagger, Dona Dinó lanced out Marcelo's eyes. She placed one of the eyeballs on the palm of her hand and held it out for the cat, smiling all the while. Osíris came running over, sniffed at the eyeball and gobbled it up. He licked his paw, his golden eyes sparkling. Dona Dinó popped the other eyeball into her own mouth and ate it as if it were an oyster, closing her eyes to savour the alkaline taste, then swallowing it whole without chewing.

The first part of the triocularity ritual was now complete

and Dona Dinó recalled what Hórus had said when he'd first introduced her to the routine:

"Remember that the eye is both mirror and mirrored. A mirror image is, by its very nature, a reflection. But the mirror image of the eye reflects an inner light. It is through this inner light that the eye sees what's on the outside. Two pairs of eyes never see the same thing in the same way. When we look at something, it is not our eyes alone that see: the Universe sees through our eyes. But only the third eye is truly creative. Zeus and Shiva are blessed with triocularity, a power that, once attained, allows us to see what others can't see. It delivers us from illusions, shams, false impressions and deceptions. It enables us to see the essence of what truly exists."

Dona Dinó began the laborious task of cutting off the dead man's head. While she worked with the sword, she said a prayer:

"Make me worthy, *São Dionísio*!"

Decapitation complete, she was ready to make the offering. She arranged the body on the bed with its arms between its thighs and placed the head in its hands. She stuck a cigarette butt into its mouth and fixed its lips into a strange smile, beneath the two empty eye sockets.

HORROR

Diamante Negro got back to the hotel at four o'clock in the morning. He went down the corridor on his tiptoes, anxious not to wake the other guests. He felt something wet and sticky on the sole of his shoe. He turned the light on to take a better look. It was blood, and it was pouring out from under Marcelo's door.

253

Diamante Negro rubbed his eyes and took a deep breath. When he opened his mouth, he choked in panic and nothing came out. He stretched his arms above his head and his body started to tremble all over. Performing a strange dance macabre, he screamed:

"*Miiiiiiinha Santa Luzia*! Help! Help!"

Stretched out on the sofa in the TV lounge, Osíris meowed, annoyed to be disturbed by the noise.